BEYOND THE TRAIL

SIX SHORT STORIES

BY JAE

Ylva

Beyond the Trail
© by Jae

ISBN epub: 978-3-95533-070-5
ISBN mobi: 978-3-95533-069-9
ISBN pdf: 978-3-95533-071-2
ISBN paperback: 978-3-95533-083-5

Published by Ylva Publishing, legal entity of Ylva Verlag, e.Kfr.

Ylva Verlag, e.Kfr.
Am Kirschgarten 2
65830 Kriftel
Germany

http://www.ylva-publishing.com

First edition: April 2013

Production and Print: Create Space

Credits
Edited by Judy Underwood, Debra Doyle, Genni Gunn, and Floyd Largent
Cover Design by Krystel Contreras (krystelc@gmail.com)
Cover Photo: © Snehitdesign | Dreamstime.com

TABLE OF CONTENTS

ACKNOWLEDGMENTS

A big thank-you goes to all the people who helped me revise and improve these short stories: my editors, Debra Doyle, Judy Underwood, Genni Gunn, and Floyd Largent, my beta reader, Pam, my critique partners, Astrid and RJ, and my test reader, Marion. Last but not least, thanks to Krystel Contreras for creating the wonderful cover.

Acknowledgements

AUTHOR'S NOTE

When I finished my novel *Backwards to Oregon*, a lot of readers asked me if I was planning on writing a sequel. I always said no. Well, that should teach me to "never say never." Not only did I write a sequel (*Hidden Truths*, which will be republished by Ylva Publishing sometime in the future), but I also wrote a number of short stories about Luke and Nora. There were so many interesting facets of the characters' lives that I couldn't explore in *Backwards to Oregon*. How and why did Luke start disguising herself as a man? How did Nora come to work in Tess's brothel? Will Tess find love too, or is she destined to spend her life alone? What happened to the Hamiltons after they reached Oregon?

This anthology answers all these questions. I hope you enjoy learning more about Luke, Nora, and Tess.

THE BLUE HOUR

Author's note

In 1838, not every state and territory celebrated Thanksgiving, and the date varied from year to year. Since the Civil War, Thanksgiving was celebrated on the fourth Thursday in November, but it was legally fixed to that date only in 1941.

Galena, Illinois
November 24th, 1838

Lucinda Hamilton laid her cheek against her skinned knees and wrapped her arms more tightly around her shins. A cold wind from the river tugged at her threadbare cape and carried the stench from the alley in her direction. She ducked her head and she buried her nose in the folds of her skirt.

From time to time, she lifted her rough hands to her mouth and breathed into them to warm her frozen fingers. Her behind felt numb, and she shifted on the top step of the backstairs.

Somewhere in the distance, the sounds of the town's busy river port drifted over—dock workers shouting at each other and a steamboat's whistle blaring. Lucinda imagined the boat loading its hold with lead from the town's mines and shipping it to a faraway place called St. Louis.

She listened for footsteps from inside the house, but none came.

What's taking so long tonight?

Lucinda stared up at the night sky, trying to guess how long she had been sitting there, waiting. The moon had set maybe an hour ago, and slowly the outlines of the brothel and the neighboring houses became distinguishable. The orange brick of the buildings looked gray in the bluish half-light. *Close to dawn already.* A wide yawn made her jaw crack, and she rubbed her eyes.

Had her mother fallen into a drunken sleep once her last customer had left, forgetting all about her?

She shifted again and shook her head. No, her mother would call her back inside in just a moment. If she was patient for a little while longer, her mother would come. *Maybe she wants to surprise me. Maybe she convinced Kate to let her have the kitchen for an hour so she can bake a pie for Thanksgiving. Or she saved up for a turkey.*

Her stomach rumbled at the thought, and she licked her cold lips.

The door behind her swung open.

Finally! Lucinda jumped up, almost tumbling down the stairs when her numb legs threatened to give out on her. But when she turned around, her gaze fell on a stranger.

A man in a long, black coat pushed past her and hurried down the stairs. Just a year or two ago, Lucinda had thought it a fun game of hide-and-seek. Now she understood that he was slinking away through the backdoor because a brothel was a place of shame.

Don't think about it. She tried to distract herself with

a familiar game, trying to guess who the visitor was. A miner? Farmer? Maybe a steamboat captain? And where was he going? Was he hurrying home to celebrate Thanksgiving with his family or attend a church service later in the day?

Lucinda wouldn't be going to church. Even if her mother felt up to going, the people of Galena wouldn't want to share a pew with a whore and her bastard child. But maybe she could slip away for a bit and watch the marksmanship contest or the horse races later in the day.

She settled back down and leaned her head against the door.

The tinny plunking of an out-of-tune piano drifted through the thin wood and mingled with footsteps.

Lucinda lifted her head away from the door as it opened again.

Another man stepped outside, one arm wrapped around Rose, keeping her pressed against his body. When they descended the stairs, he palmed Rose's behind.

She inched to the side to let them pass and stared at her boots until his footsteps faded away.

Rose climbed the stairs and sat next to her on the top step. Two coins clinked when she slid them into her low-cut bodice, making Lucinda wonder what she wore underneath.

Quickly, she shoved the thought away.

"What are you doin' out here?" Rose asked. "It's dangerous for a girl all alone out here."

"Not more dangerous than inside, is it? At least out here, it's quiet."

Rose sighed. "How long have you been sittin' here? Don't tell me that goddamned Lilly forgot all about you again?"

"Oh, no, she'll call me back in as soon as the last guest is gone."

Rose's full lips twitched, but she said nothing. She smoothed her hands over her skirt, which was so short that the storeowner's wife had called it a scandal last week. "Come on, honey," Rose said and stood. "You can keep me company for a li'l while."

The warm air in the brothel made Lucinda's cold cheeks burn as if hit by a thousand pinpricks. She stumbled along the corridor, her boots sinking into a carpet that had been royal red when she had first seen it five years ago. Now its color had faded to a tired rust brown.

From the first floor, the clinking of glasses and shouts from the faro table drifted up the stairs. "It's almost morning," Lucinda said. "Why aren't the men going home?"

"Kate will keep the parlor open all night and all day tomorrow." Rose shrugged. "Said the Thanksgiving crowd will bring in some extra money."

Lucinda's shoulders slumped. How much longer until she could crawl into bed and finally find a few hours of sleep?

Rose opened a door and tugged on her sleeve. "I'm done for the night. You can come in and share my bed." A broken-off front tooth flashed when she giggled. "Didn't think I'd say that again tonight."

Blood rushed to Lucinda's cheeks, and she turned her face away. She sat on the edge of the bed. Like her mother's room, this one had no other place to sit.

The sound of water splashing made her look up.

Rose dipped a cloth into the washbowl and rubbed it over her face. Beneath a heavy mask of rouge, a pale face appeared.

Try as she might, Lucinda couldn't stop staring, even as Rose turned and looked at her. She had always thought of Rose as her mother's friend. Well, not friend, really, but someone who shared her history. Now, after seeing her without the rouge, she realized that Rose was barely older than fifteen or sixteen. But where Lucinda was gangly and still flat-chested, Rose was elegant and pleasantly rounded. The weary expression in her eyes said she'd seen and done things that Lucinda had only listened to through the protection of closed doors.

In three or four years, this could be me. The thought rippled through her, shaking her.

"What?" Rose asked, one hand resting on her hip.

Lucinda wrenched her gaze away. "Nothing."

"Nothing?" Rose flicked water at her. "Then why are you starin' at me like I'm a cow with two heads?"

"It's just that ..." A drop of water ran down Lucinda's chin, and she wiped it away. "You're beautiful."

Rose laughed—not the fake laugh Lucinda had heard her use to entice men but a deep chuckle that flowed over her like a cleansing rain. "Thank you, honey," Rose said. "You're a real sweetheart." Then her grin dimmed, and she shook her head. "Your mother shouldn't have brought you here. This hellhole is no place for you."

The edge of the bed dug into Lucinda's hands when she clamped her fingers around it. She kept her gaze focused on her knuckles. "I know." She glanced up at Rose, then away. "It's no place for you or any other woman either."

"I'm stayin' just until I earn enough to start a new life," Rose said.

A burning sensation spread down Lucinda's throat until it settled in her stomach. She'd heard those words before. In fact, her mother had said them in every town, every new brothel, and every night Lucinda had to wait outside their room.

She hasn't said it in a while. She realized her mother had stopped talking about getting out. Now she just worried about getting enough whiskey and laudanum to make it through the night.

"Come on." Rose slid out of her colorful skirt and tight bodice and stood before her in just a see-through shift. "Let's go to bed."

"Um." Lucinda slammed her eyes shut. The thought of sharing the bed with Rose made her uncomfortable. Somehow, it felt different from sharing the bed with her mother. "I-I think I'll go see if Mama has finished entertaining for tonight." She escaped from the room before Rose could stop her.

Wandering down the hall, she ignored the noises—snores, grunts, and moans—coming from behind the doors as best as she could. She stopped in front of the room she shared with her mother and pressed her ear against the door.

Nothing.

No grunts, no heavy breathing, not even her mother's drunken snores.

Lucinda blew out a breath. Maybe her mother had stopped working to spend some time with her. Maybe she'd already been looking for her. She opened the door an inch at a time, ready to stop and retreat should a customer still be with her mother.

Everything stayed quiet.

She slipped into the room.

The sickening mix of stale liquor, sweat, and cheap perfume hit her nose.

Lucinda gagged and crossed the room to open the

window. In the dim light, she almost stumbled over a pair of boots. The oil lamp on the scarred dresser flickered and dimmed as the oil in the reservoir burned low.

Lucinda turned and looked at her mother.

Lilly lay on the bed, the violet coverlet rumpled around her. The red ruffles of her skirt had slipped up one thigh, revealing one of her garters. A bottle of whiskey had slid from her hand and spilled its content onto the floor.

Quickly, Lucinda crossed the room and picked up the bottle. It was empty now anyway.

When she straightened, her gaze fell onto an empty vial clutched in her mother's hand. She wrinkled her nose as she caught the heavy odor of laudanum. *Not again.* She sighed.

There'd be no talking to her mother tonight. Her mother would spend Thanksgiving floating in numb lethargy, leaving Lucinda behind.

She dragged the covers up over her mother. When she tucked them around her, cold skin brushed her fingers. "Mama?" Lucinda whispered. She bent closer.

Her mother didn't move. Didn't breathe.

Dread clutched Lucinda, squeezing until she couldn't breathe either.

"Mama!" She shook her mother's shoulder. "Mama, please!"

The empty vial slid from beneath a limp hand and rolled onto the floor.

With trembling fingers, Lucinda felt for a pulse.

Nothing.

She pressed one hand to her mouth and bit back a sob. When her knees threatened to give out, she sank to the floor and rested her back against the bed. "Lord, Mama, what did you do? What did you do?" Numbness spread through her, as if she, not Mama, had drunk the laudanum. She rubbed burning eyes, but no tears would come.

When the sun peeked over the horizon, Lucinda struggled to her feet. She stood looking down at her mother, then lifted a hand and trailed a finger over rouged cheeks and painted eyebrows, a touch her mother hadn't allowed when she was alive.

Outside, a door banged shut.

Lucinda flinched. She straightened, turned away from her mother, and went to tell Kate.

* * *

Kate read haltingly, stumbling over a word every so often. Finally, she said "amen" and closed the Bible.

Unclamping her lips, Lucinda mumbled "amen" too. She knew at least that much of the Lord's Prayer from attending other funerals. Just last month, Fanny, who had the room next to theirs, had been choked to death by a customer.

Now half a dozen of the brothel's girls had dragged themselves out of bed to say good-bye to Lilly, but no pastor was present. He had refused to bury Lilly in the cemetery's sacred soil, so Kate had paid someone to dig a grave near a lone crossroad at the edge of town.

Lucinda stared at the wooden cross on her mother's grave. Because she couldn't afford a granite tombstone, someone had carved her mother's name into a simple cross. Now the wood held two of the few words Lucinda could read.

Lilly Hamilton.

Was that even her mother's real name? Lucinda wasn't sure. Most of the women in brothels didn't use their real names, so there were lots of Daisys, Roses, and Lillys in the parlor houses, cribs, and bordellos. If her mother had ever been called by another name, it was long forgotten.

A hand on her shoulder made Lucinda jerk.

"What are you gonna do now?" Kate asked. She hooked her arm through Lucinda's and set them off toward the brothel.

Lucinda dug her teeth into her lip. "Don't know."

"Got no relatives that can take you in?"

"No." Her father was one of many faceless customers who had shared her mother's bed, and Lucinda had never known her grandparents. She was on her own now. Her belly cramped into a ball of anxiety at the thought.

Around the bend, the brothel's orange brick façade appeared in her line of sight.

"How old are you now?" Kate asked.

"Just turned twelve."

Kate studied her like a side of bacon she wanted to buy. "You're welcome to stay on, you know. With a bit of rouge and some cotton padding in your corset, you could be quite pretty."

Lucinda stared at her, took in the madam's grim face, the thin lips turned down as if she were constantly tasting something bitter. The rouge couldn't hide the broken blood vessels across Kate's nose and plump cheeks. "No," Lucinda choked out through a tight throat. *No. Not that. Never that.*

Kate shrugged. "Suit yourself. But don't come back crying when you realize that a girl alone won't get very far."

* * *

Lucinda packed her only other dress and put the hairbrush in her carpetbag but left her mother's bottle of perfume. When she closed the bag, her glance fell onto the mirror shard on her mother's dresser. A customer had broken the mirror some months ago, but Lilly didn't have the money to replace it.

Outside, horses raced by the brothel and riders shouted, trying to win the Thanksgiving contest. She knew many of the riders. More than just a few were regular customers, and she had always envied the freedom that being men gave them. No one ever spoke ill of them for visiting the brothel. No one criticized them for racing horses or doing whatever else they wanted.

A girl alone won't get very far. Kate's words echoed through her mind.

She knew Kate was right. What options did she have for survival? She couldn't read or write and had no talent for needlework. The one thing she was good at was taking care of the two horses Kate kept in the town's livery stable.

But no one would hire a girl to work in a stable. Stable boys were just that—boys.

A girl alone.

She trailed her hands through her long, black tresses. Years ago, some of the younger prostitutes had oohed and aahed over them, combing Lucinda's hair as if she were a doll. While she had liked the attention, she'd never been that fond of her long hair.

What if ...? She gathered her hair behind her head and stared at herself in the broken mirror.

Not allowing herself time to reconsider, she picked up a pair of scissors.

Black locks fell onto the dresser, and she imagined

stripping off the grief, anger, and shame of her past with them. When she was done, she wiped the strands of hair away from the mirror and stared at the thin, pale boy looking back at her. She touched the bare skin of her neck and slid her palms down her still flat chest.

Could this really work? Would she be able to make people believe she was a boy?

She tried a male pose, her thumbs stuck in imaginary vest pockets, but it looked out of place since she was wearing a dress. Another idea came to her and made her smile. When she looked down, the boy in the mirror answered with a grin of his own.

She opened her mother's trunk. Beneath half-empty bottles of whiskey, she found a man's shirt and pants. One of her mother's customers had liked for Lilly to dress up as a boy.

After slipping her dress over her head, she stepped into the pants, pulled them up, and rolled up the too-long pant legs. The waistband was too loose, so she was grateful for the suspenders that held the pants in place on her narrow hips. The shirt was too wide at the shoulders, but it would conceal whatever female form she had.

She glanced in the mirror again, blinked, and shook her head at her image. *This is me!*

It felt as if she were seeing herself for the first time.

Her gaze swept through the room, taking it all in one last time, then she picked up her bag, turned, and strode away.

* * *

The door opened just as Lucinda wanted to give up knocking. A sleepy Rose, wrapped in a short dressing gown, blinked at her. "For heaven's sake, it's the middle of the day. Come back tonight." Already closing the door, she asked, "Besides, aren't you a bit young to lie with a woman?"

"What?" Almost too late, Lucinda held out her hands and stopped the door from closing. "Oh. No, no. That's not why ... Rose, it's me."

The door whooshed open so abruptly that Lucinda stumbled into the room. Rose caught her, then held her at arms' length and stared at her. "Lucinda?"

She nodded and, trying to make her voice sound firm like a boy's, added, "I suppose you should use another name now. Call me ... Luke."

"Luke?" Rose's brow contracted. "What are you doing?"

The unfamiliar shirt slid against her skin as she straightened her shoulders. "Starting a new life."

"As a boy?" Rose's carefully tended eyebrows arched.

"It feels right."

Rose let her gaze wander down Luke's body, making her blush. "Looks right too," she said with a shake of her head. "Except ..."

"What?" Luke peered down her body but couldn't find anything amiss. As far as she could tell, she looked like every other twelve-year-old boy in Galena.

"Well, you're missing somethin'."

Luke smoothed her palm over the back of her neck and through her hair. "You mean a hat?"

"That too." Grinning, Rose glanced down Luke's body. "Take off your pants."

Heat stained Luke's cheeks. "What? No. Why?" She clamped her hands around the suspenders, tightly holding on.

20

Rose rolled her eyes. She turned away, searched for something in her dresser, and then strode over to Luke. Before Luke could react, Rose stuffed her hand down her pants.

"Rose!" She struggled to get away, but Rose was stronger. "W-what are you doing?"

"Calm down. I'm not out to hurt you. There." Finally, Rose withdrew her hand. When she glanced down at the spot between Luke's legs, she gave a satisfied nod.

Her heart still hammering against her ribs, Luke followed Rose's gaze down.

A soft object tented the material at the crotch of her pants. Luke carefully touched it. The tips of her ears burned. "W-what's that?"

"Don't worry." Rose laughed. "It won't bite your privates. Just some rolled-up stockings. Now you can pass as a boy." She shook her head and stared at Luke. "And a handsome one at that."

More heat suffused Luke's cheeks, and she frowned at herself. *Boys don't blush about things like this. If you want this to work, you better stop acting like a girl.*

"So you're leavin'?" Rose asked.

Luke nodded. "I'll try to get hired as a stable boy."

"Sure beats the only other option," Rose mumbled. "But you'll get older. Your bosom will grow, and you'll start your monthly curses. What will you do then?"

Luke's mother had talked to her about these things, but somehow, imagining herself as a woman was stranger than wearing men's apparel. She raked her front teeth over her bottom lip. "I'll think of something." She held out her hand. "Good-bye, Rose."

Instead of taking her hand, Rose pulled her close for a short hug. "Take care of yourself," she whispered. "I'm glad you're gettin' out of here. That's at least somethin' to be thankful for at Thanksgivin'."

"You could come with me," Luke said. With Rose at her side, leaving the brothel and Galena wouldn't be quite so scary. She imagined earning enough money to buy a turkey for the two of them next Thanksgiving.

"I don't think my bosom is as easy to hide." Rose lifted one side of her mouth into a crooked grin.

"You wouldn't need to." Luke gestured down her body, at the men's clothes. "I could take care of you."

Rose's half-grin blossomed into a true smile. "Thanks, honey. You're quite the gentleman already. As much as I hate livin' here, I don't think I'm cut out for a life like you're plannin'. Always hidin' ..." She shook her head.

Luke nodded, but strangely, she didn't feel as if she were hiding. For the first time in her life, she wasn't ducking her head.

As she made her way downstairs, heading for the front door instead of slinking out the back, a few customers were still standing at the pockmarked bar with its row of spittoons, celebrating Thanksgiving in their own way. Luke hoped that one day, she'd have something to be thankful for too.

###

GRASPING AT STRAWS

Independence, Missouri
June 15th, 1847

A pitchfork of soiled straw and horse apples almost hit Tess in the face.

"Hey!" Tess flattened herself against one of the stalls. "Watch where you throw that!"

Willie, the stable boy, grazed her with an indifferent glance. "Sorry," he said, not even trying to sound as if he meant it. Without another look at her, he continued to muck the stalls.

Tess's gloved fingers tightened into a fist. This wasn't the first time Willie had treated her so rudely. He never fetched her horse for her, never helped her into or out of the saddle, and never greeted her when she entered the stable. He knew that as a fallen woman, she had no way to enforce a more respectful treatment.

Or so he thought.

A smile curved Tess's lips as she marched down the center aisle between two rows of stalls. *Little does he know that it's me who's paying his wages.* She passed one of the stalls, and her gaze fell on the water trough. Bits of straw and manure drifted on a murky sludge that had once been fresh water.

Seems he doesn't have any more respect for the horses

than he does for me. She sent a sharp glance back at the young man. *Fool.* Her next stop would be her business partner's office. Before the day ended, Willie would be an unemployed fool.

This was just the last straw. She had talked to Donovan about Willie's carelessness before, but whatever action Donovan had taken apparently hadn't changed Willie's work ethic.

Tess continued down the aisle, checking the condition of the horses and stalls. Many of the stalls were empty. Business was slow, not just for the stable but for the brothel too. The masses of emigrants heading west had left Independence weeks ago, and the soldiers stationed at nearby Fort Leavenworth were still fighting in Mexico.

A picture of Luke's earnest gray eyes flashed through her mind, and Tess sent a quick prayer to whatever God might be willing to listen to a whore. *Please, keep Luke safe.* Then she shoved the thought away. Her life had no room for sentimentalities.

She reached out to open her mare's stall when something caught her attention.

In the empty stall next to her, right at the end of the aisle, straw rustled.

Probably just a mouse stealing some corn for supper.

But the warning tingle at the back of her neck kept her hand suspended over the stall door. Tess had learned to trust her instincts.

There!

The rustle sounded again. Something scraped against the wooden wall.

Tess tensed. The Deringer under her riding skirts rested comfortably against her thigh.

Tess's mare flicked her ears in the direction of the

sounds but didn't seem alarmed. Obviously, the mare was familiar with whatever was moving around in that stall.

Maybe just a cat. Tess took two quick steps and peered over the stall door.

The eyes that stared back at her didn't belong to a cat. In one corner of the stall, a young woman huddled behind the feeding trough.

Tess's hand fluttered to her chest. She opened her mouth for a surprised shout.

"No," the young woman whispered. "Please. Don't give me away. I have nowhere else to go."

"So you're living in my stable, stealing food from the horses?" Tess pointed at the brownish carrot clenched in the girl's hand.

The girl hung her head. A mass of fiery red hair escaped from under a weather-beaten sunbonnet and fell like a curtain around her face.

Heavy boots trudged toward them. "Who are you talking to?" Willie shouted down the aisle.

The girl's head flew up. She stared at Tess with wide eyes. Her full lips formed a silent "Oh, no."

Tess calmly turned around. "Just talking to myself. You know how we womenfolk are."

Willie spat out his stalk of straw and grunted in agreement. After one last glance back over his shoulder, he grabbed the handles of the wheelbarrow and pushed it out of the stable.

When he had disappeared around the corner, Tess turned back around and beckoned to the red-haired girl still clinging to the feeding trough. "Come out of there."

"Please, don't throw me out," the girl said. She didn't move from her hiding place. "Just one night. I promise I'll be gone by the morning."

"And then?" Tess asked. "Where will you go?" She shook her head at herself. *What do you care? Don't you have enough girls to worry about?*

The girl's slender shoulders slumped for a moment and then straightened. "I don't know, but I'll find a way." Determination gleamed in her eyes.

Find a way. In a town like Independence, there were few ways for a woman to survive on her own. Tess knew it better than anyone else did. Over the years, she had taken in more young women down on their luck than she could count. *But not right now.* At the moment, she could ill afford to feed another hungry mouth.

The girl shifted and rose from behind the feeding trough.

Tess's glance fell on her swollen belly. *Oh, Lord.* She sighed. *Make that two hungry mouths.*

For a moment, she wondered how the young woman, pregnant and all alone, had made it to Independence. Judging by the way she spoke, she had grown up in a well-off family back east. Even the worn clothing and the hungry look in the girl's eyes couldn't hide her manners and good education.

Same old story. Tess sighed. *I bet her family threw her out when they discovered she was going to have a child out of wedlock.*

The girl followed Tess's gaze and covered her belly with soft-looking hands. "You said 'my stable.' Does that mean you own all this?" Awe and skepticism mingled in her voice.

Tess gave a tired nod. *I wonder if there'll ever come a time when people won't raise their eyebrows at the thought of women owning a business.*

The girl inched closer but stayed out of touching

distance.

She doesn't trust people. Lately, Tess had wondered whether, after so many years of working in brothels, she had lost the ability to care about people. First Luke and now this young woman were proving her wrong. She knew better than to ask about the girl's past, though. Maybe that was why the girl had come west. People here tended to ask fewer questions.

"If you own the stable," the girl glanced up at her, hope dancing in her eyes, "then maybe you need someone to sweep the floor and—"

"Girl," Tess said. "While I need a new stable boy, this is no work for a woman, especially not a woman who's with child." The citizens of Independence would never accept a female caring for their horses, and business was dragging as it was.

"Then maybe—"

"The only job I have to offer is not something that you'd want," Tess said.

The girl's green eyes flashed. "I'll do anything it takes." She pressed her hands against her belly.

Tess took in the red hair, the pretty face, and the porcelain skin. Underneath streaks of dirt and patched-up clothes, beauty was just waiting to be discovered. The young woman would bring in good money for the brothel once she was no longer with child. "No," Tess said to the girl and to herself. "Not anything."

"Yes." The girl held eye contact. "Anything."

The hopeful gaze resting on her sparked Tess's anger. "Don't look at me like I'm your salvation. Don't you know who I am? What I am? Don't you know why the stable boy can get away with throwing horse apples at me?"

The girl blinked.

"Oh, for Christ's sake, don't you understand? I'm a whore, girl. I own a brothel, and that's the only job I can offer you." She already had a cook and a woman to take care of the laundry, both former prostitutes who had become too old to entice men. She couldn't afford to take in more women who didn't earn their keep.

Russet lashes lowered, and a blush spread over the girl's fair skin. "Oh."

Tess swallowed against the bitter taste in her mouth. "Yeah. Oh."

When the blush receded, the girl looked up and met Tess's eyes. "Anything it takes," the girl said again.

Guilt swept over Tess, and suddenly, she was the one who had to look away. Could she really condemn this young woman to a life like hers? But then again, was sleeping in stables and stealing food any better? If someone like Willie found her, there was no telling what would happen to the defenseless girl. At least if she kept an eye on them, the unborn baby would have a chance to survive.

Tess stepped closer, and this time, the girl didn't move away but stood her ground.

"All right," Tess said. "But if you work for me, there are rules involved." She forced herself to focus on being a businesswoman.

"Don't steal your silverware?" A mischievous grin danced over the girl's face, then disappeared as she waited for Tess's reaction to her quip.

Tess smiled. *She's got spunk. Good.* It would help her survive life in a brothel. "Be discreet," Tess said. "Keeping their secrets is what gives us power over our customers. A loose tongue can get you killed."

The girl nodded earnestly.

Tess felt another twinge of guilt. "And you best not get any romantic notions about falling in love with a customer and being carried off to start a new life. That very rarely happens."

Once again, the girl nodded. Her full lips formed a line of pain but then quickly relaxed when she realized Tess was still watching her.

She's gonna be good at the kind of work we do. Maybe too good. Tess hoped the girl would grab at the first chance to leave the brothel and find something else she was good at.

"Don't worry," the girl said. "Love is not for me."

Tess had heard that before. Luke had told her the exact same thing when Tess had warned her not to fall in love with her just because they shared a bed.

"All right." Tess gave her a grim smile and opened the stall door separating them. "Last chance to change your mind."

Instead of answering, the girl stepped out into the aisle. One of her hands still rested on her belly. "Whatever it takes," she said again.

Tess sighed. "Then let's go before Willie returns." She grasped the girl's elbow and led her out of the stable.

Before they stepped out onto the street, the girl paused. "Thank you."

"Don't thank me. I'm not sure I'm doing you any favors." Already, Tess began to regret her decision. The burden of responsibility rested heavily on her. Maybe she could find some light housework for the young woman until the baby was born, but after that, Tess couldn't afford to let her stay if she didn't entertain customers.

Faces of regulars appeared before her mind's eye,

but she discarded them as too rough. For a moment, she thought of Luke and then laughed at herself. *Aren't you forgetting a little something?* No, it was better to keep the girl away from Luke. She didn't trust anyone else with Luke's secret.

When they paused to let a wagon pass, the girl offered her hand. "Nora Macauley."

"Tess Swenson." Tess laid her hand into the unexpectedly firm grip of the girl. "I think," she said as she steered Nora toward her new home, "you should use the name 'Fleur.'"

"Fleur? Why Fleur?"

It certainly wasn't because their customers were refined gentlemen fluent in French, but maybe Nora didn't need to know that just yet. "Maybe because 'straw' wouldn't sound as enticing as 'flower,'" she said and plucked one of the yellow stalks out of Nora's hair.

Nora smiled. "Fleur it is."

Her smile was contagious, and Tess hoped Nora would never completely lose the sparkle in her eyes. "Come on. Hurry," she said and crossed the street, "I have a stable boy to fire."

###

A Rooster's Job

A gust of wind rattled the greased paper that covered the windows instead of glass. Snow drifted down the chimney, and the flames flickered and hissed.

Luke stepped around her oldest daughter, Amy, and her herd of wooden horses and laid a fresh log on the fire, thankful for something to do. In the year since she, Nora, and the children had arrived in Oregon, temperatures had never before dropped so low. She was glad to have chopped and dried enough wood for the winter. They could keep warm at least.

"Papa, can you make me a baby horse for Measles?" Amy asked, eyeing the wood at the side of the hearth.

Luke had whittled her a menagerie of animals to mirror the ones on their property, but her five-year-old daughter liked the horses best, especially Measles, who was supposed to have a foal in spring.

"Tonight," Luke said. "I need to—"Another weak cough came from the bedroom. *Oh, Nattie.* The strangled sound made Luke's chest ache as if she had been coughing and wheezing for the past two days. She thought about returning to the bedroom to stand silent vigil with Nora

31

over their sick daughter but then stayed where she was. It hurt too much to watch the tiny chest struggle for breath.

If only they didn't live so far from a doctor. If only the snow melted.

Suddenly, Luke couldn't breathe either. The walls of the small cabin were closing in on her. She grabbed her coat and rushed to the door.

"Papa!" Amy laid down her wooden horses and jumped up from her place next to the hearth. "Can I come too?"

She was used to going everywhere with Luke, and normally, Luke liked to have her around and to teach her new things. But not now, not in this weather. She wouldn't risk Amy getting sick too.

"No. Not this time."

"But we could check on Measles and the other horses," Amy said.

"No," Luke said again, more roughly than she had intended. "It's too cold outside. Tell your mother I'm going to take care of the roof." Without another word, she escaped from the cabin.

The cold hit her like a tidal wave, but Luke ignored it and marched toward the stable. After one step, she sank knee-deep into the snow. She struggled through the white drifts, her fists clenched in the pockets of her coat.

When she entered the barn, half a dozen horses trumpeted a hopeful whinny.

Luke bit her lip. She didn't have feed to offer them. As she made her way down the aisle, she forced herself not to look at the empty stalls. She reached over one of the stall doors and rubbed her hand over Measles's shoulder, feeling bones more prominent than ever before. "I'm sorry, girl," she whispered. "I'm so sorry. I'll go out later and get you some more moss from the forest."

But first, she had to knock down some of the snow from the cabin and stable roofs before they caved in under their heavy burden. Oregon's winters were normally mild and rainy, so Luke hadn't built their home with so much snow in mind. The cabin wasn't much more than provisional shelter anyway. Lichen grew on the log walls, and Nora had to sweep mushrooms off the dirt floor every morning.

Luke had planned on installing wood floors in the new, better house she had wanted to build during their first summer in Oregon. But now that summer had passed and with so much else to do around the ranch, she hadn't gotten around to it. "Never mind," Jacob Garfield, their old friend whose family had settled in town, had said. "You'll build a new house next year. You can't do it all at once. After all, you're just one man."

Her callused hand rasped over her burning eyes. *You're no man at all.* In the past year, she had found peace with that fact, but now it started to feel like a failure again. If she were a man, maybe she could have built a better home, one with real windows and a cook stove so Nora wouldn't need to cook over a fire anymore. Maybe then Nattie wouldn't be sick all the time. If she didn't have to hide her secret, they could have settled down in town, with neighbors and a doctor nearby, instead of living isolated from the rest of the world.

Sometimes, Luke feared that Nora was lonely without even a post office from which to send her letters to Tess. Could she really give Nora and her daughters the life they deserved? In moments like this, she doubted it.

The rafters above her creaked warningly.

Dammit. I better hurry. Luke carried a ladder outside, leaned it against the side of the stable, and climbed up. A cold wind tugged on her coat. Her fingers felt frozen as she used a shovel to relieve the stable's roof of its burden. Snow slithered into her coat sleeves and dripped down her neck as she worked, but she ignored it. Every shovelful seemed to weigh a ton, and sweat mingled with the melting snow on her skin.

Finally, she freed the roof of most of the snow and climbed back down. Her arms protested as she dragged the ladder through the deep snow toward the cabin. Despite her exhaustion, she couldn't allow herself to rest. She would need to chop more wood, go out to set traps in the forest, and drag home moss so the horses wouldn't starve.

More white drifted across the ranch yard.

Luke frowned and stopped. *That's not snow. Lord! Are those feathers?*

Then she saw the drops of crimson that marred the treacherous innocence of the snow. The ladder slid out of her nerveless hands. She bent down and touched one of the spots, confirming that it was blood.

Fear clutched at her as she followed the trail of blood around the corner. She already knew where it was leading. *No. Please, no. Not this too.* When she ducked into the henhouse, unusual silence greeted her.

It was empty.

Broken eggshells and tufts of bloodstained feathers littered the floor. On the perch, the battered-looking rooster flapped his wings helplessly.

Luke stared at him. Bile rose in her throat; she forced it down. "You should have taken better care of your family," she said. "That's your job, you stupid rooster."

The rooster just crowed at her.

"Goddammit!" Luke yelled back. She rubbed her palms over her cold face until her cheeks burned.

A coyote had gotten into the henhouse before, but that had been last year, when the winter had been mild. This year had brought the hardest winter that settlers in Oregon could remember. The river was frozen, and eighteen inches of snow covered the pasture. Half their herd and two of their milk cows had starved because they couldn't get to the grass. They had run out of flour a week ago, but the snow blocked the roads and made it impossible to reach town. Even if they had somehow managed to make it to the store, prices had soared, so they couldn't afford to buy more than a few pounds anyway.

All Luke could do was hope for spring to come soon.

She jerked the board that had come loose next to the henhouse's door back into place and waded through the snow to where she had left the ladder. There was no time to think about what losing the hens would mean for them or what Nora would say when she heard about it. The cabin's roof was flat, so the snow wouldn't slide off. If she didn't clear it, it would pile higher and higher until the roof caved in and exposed Luke's family to the merciless elements.

Anger fueled her strength, and she shoveled wildly until she had scraped most of the snow off the cabin's cedar shakes. Then she paused, still clinging to the ladder, and stared down at the snow-immersed corral, the feathers, and the trail of blood.

* * *

Nora shoved open the door and tucked her shawl more tightly around her shoulders. "Luke?" she called out into the white, frozen world. What was Luke doing out there for so long? Had something happened?

"Up here," Luke called from the side of the cabin. "Go on back inside. I'll be down in a minute." Her voice sounded strangely hollow to Nora.

Nora furrowed her brow. Was it just the snow, which muffled and distorted all sounds? She didn't think so. "Luke?" Nora called again, with more urgency. She stepped out of the doorway, let the door fall closed behind her, and peered up.

The ladder leaned against the cabin, with Luke perched on top.

Luke scrambled down the ladder, her cheeks flushed with panic. "Is Nattie ...?"

"No, no, she's fine," Nora said and waved at Luke to slow down before she could fall and break a leg. "Her fever finally broke, and she's no longer coughing. She'll be just—" The words died on her lips, and she stared at the tears that pooled in the corners of Luke's red-rimmed eyes. Her heart plummeted. "Are you ... are you crying?"

In the two years she'd known Luke, through a lot of hard times, she had never, ever seen Luke cry. Even when one of the horses had stepped on Luke's little toe and crushed it, she had bravely upheld her manly image. She had cursed but never cried—until now.

"No," Luke said, quickly wiping her eyes. "Of course not. It's this damn cold. It makes my eyes water."

Her attempts to hide her feelings hurt as much as seeing Luke suffer, but Nora let it go. Right now, making sure that Luke was all right was more important. "What happened?" She touched Luke's hand. The gentle strength of that hand had comforted and loved her for many months now, but this time, Luke didn't curl her fingers around hers in silent communication. They remained frozen.

What's going on? Nora studied Luke more closely.

Her eyes widened as she detected the red stains on Luke's coat sleeve. "Lord! You're hurt." Her insides trembled, and she reached for Luke's hand again.

"No." Now Luke intertwined her fingers with Nora's, instinctively soothing. "It's not my blood. It's ..." Luke closed her eyes, and when she opened them again, she looked toward the henhouse.

Her silence said it all.

"The chickens?" Nora whispered. "All of them?"

"All but that goddamn useless rooster."

Nora took a deep breath. Then another. "Well," she finally said and forced a smile, "I bet he's not so useless when it comes to preparing chicken fixings. We could have potatoes, steamed squash, and turnips with it." That was about all that was left in their pantry—that and the can of peaches Nora was saving for Luke's birthday.

Her words didn't have the desired effect. Luke didn't smile; she didn't even make eye contact. "As soon as the snow melts away a little, you and the girls should move to town," Luke said. "I'm sure you could stay with the Garfields for a while."

"What?"

"Just until spring." Under Nora's incredulous gaze, Luke shuffled her booted feet. "Just until I can build a better house for us."

A sigh formed a cloud of mist in front of Nora's face. "Luke, we talked about this before. The answer is still no."

"But before, we hadn't lost the hens and two of the cows," Luke said.

Nora was still shaking her head. Now that she had found a home and the love of her life, she wouldn't leave either of them.

Snow sprayed both of them when Luke kicked one of the white drifts. "What else needs to happen before you leave?" The normally gentle Luke was shouting now.

"You'd have to leave too," Nora said without flinching back. "We're either all going or all staying. I'm not leaving you behind. Through the good times and the bad, remember?"

Luke stared down into the snow and mumbled into her coat, "You made that promise when you still thought I was a man who could take care of you and the girls."

"I'm not talking about our marriage vows," Nora said. Back then, she'd had no earthly clue about love. She'd married Luke to give her children a better future in a new home. But somewhere along the two thousand miles from Missouri to Oregon, she had fallen in love. "Do you remember last year, when we stopped the oxen on that hill over there and looked down at this very place? Do you remember what I said?"

Luke's gaze wandered over to the hill hidden beneath the heavy snow cover, then came to rest on Nora. For a moment, her eyes were alight with the memory and a slight smile trembled on her lips. "Of course I do. You told me you'd love me forever, through the good times and the bad, until the end of time."

"That I did. And while this," Nora swept her arm over the frozen landscape, "might look like the Last Days, I'm sure it's not, so my promise still holds true." She reached out and touched Luke's cheek, feeling the dampness of sweat, snow—and, yes, tears. "Luke, what's this about? What's going on in here?" She slid her hand down the thick coat and rested it on one bound breast, directly over Luke's heart.

Two cold hands closed around Nora's. "I just want you

to be safe. It would be better for you and the girls to live in a real house and have flour and eggs and milk. I can't give you any of that right now." Luke dropped her hands from Nora's and looked away.

"And you somehow think people in town and on the other farms aren't suffering this winter? Most of our neighbors lost more stock than we did." Just a few days before, Luke had found two of the Buchanans' cows dead on their north pasture. At least they would provide meat for both families for a while. "These things are out of your control, Luke. There would be nothing you could do about them even if you were a man. Or do you think that Jacob or Tom would be able to melt away the snow with just the heat of their manly gazes?"

"Of course not," Luke said, but her guarded expression never changed.

Lord. Why did I have to go and marry such a pigheaded person? Nora smiled inwardly. *Maybe because she's also such an honorable and loving person.* "Luke, things aren't that bad. So what if we have to eat potatoes, turnips, and boiled wheat for a few weeks longer? We have more than enough food to survive this winter. It just won't be the most varied of cuisine." She nudged Luke, trying to establish eye contact. "If we run out of beef, you could go out and hunt. I hear the coyotes are well-nourished around here."

The corners of Luke's gray eyes crinkled as her concerned features relaxed into a tentative smile.

"And spring comes early here in Oregon," Nora added. "The snow could be gone by the New Year, and then everything will look different."

The cabin's door creaked open. "Mama? Papa?" Amy's worried voice drifted over to them.

"We're here, Amy," Nora said.

Amy leaned forward, both hands clutching the doorway, and peered at them, her lower body still within the cabin. They had forbidden her from setting one foot outside the cabin without them, and Amy was taking that order very seriously. Her eyes widened. "Papa, are you all right?"

"Yes, sweetie, I'm—"

Nora knew what was coming. She had heard that reassurance a thousand times before. Most of the time, Nora thought a little white lie to avoid worrying the children was fine, but she didn't want Luke to think that she had to pretend all the time. "Papa is sad because the hens are gone," she said before Luke could finish her sentence.

"Oh, no!" Amy's happy little face transformed into a frowning one. "What happened to them?"

"I'll explain later," Nora said. "Now go back inside where it's warm. Be a dear and keep an eye on your sister. We'll be with you in a minute."

After a second's hesitation, Amy closed the door.

Luke and Nora were left standing in the snow, staring at each other. More snowflakes dusted Luke's shoulders, and Nora brushed them away. "You are a hard worker, a wonderful parent, and the best husband I could wish for," Nora said. "But I don't expect you to have all the answers and all the solutions for every problem. I won't think any less of you if you don't know what to do every once in a while. You don't have to be strong all the time."

"But if I don't—"

One finger against Luke's bluish lips stopped the words. "We'll figure it out together, all right?" Nora took her hand away and waited.

Luke exhaled sharply, and the forming cloud mingled with Nora's condensed breath.

The image made Nora smile. She bridged the space between them and pressed her lips to Luke's. "All right?" she asked again.

"All right," Luke whispered against her lips.

* * *

Luke leaned in the doorway, one arm wrapped tightly around Nora, and watched Nattie sleep. The rhythmic movements of the covers lulled her heart to a calmer beat. Finally, she let herself believe that everything would be all right. She vowed to get started on the new house as soon as the snow melted away and the ground dried.

"Here, Papa," Amy said next to her. "For you."

Something was slid into her hand, and Luke instinctively curled her fingers around it. She looked down into Amy's earnest green eyes.

"Don't be sad about the hens, Papa. You can have one of my animals."

Luke lifted the wooden animal to study it in the dim light filtering in from the fireplace. It wasn't just any of Amy's carved animals. Her fingers rubbed over the tiny spots on the horse's flank. "Measles," Luke said. Her throat constricted. A soft squeeze from Nora finally propelled her into action. She let go of Nora and knelt down to be at eye level with Amy. "Thank you, Amy," she said. Her voice trembled. *Get yourself together. You can't let her see you—*Then she paused and glanced at Nora's hand resting on her shoulder.

You don't have to be strong all the time, Nora had said. *I won't think any less of you.*

"I can't take your horse from you, sweetie," Luke said.

Amy reached out, about to take her beloved toy horse, but then she stopped and looked back and forth between Luke and the wooden animal. After one last longing glance at the horse figure, she pulled back her hand. "But I don't want you to be sad."

"Know what would make me feel better?"

"A hug?"

Luke nodded. "A big hug from you."

With a squeal, Amy threw herself into Luke's arms.

The trusting warmth of Amy's small body made Luke close her eyes. *Maybe,* she thought as she laid her cheek against Amy's soft curls, *maybe I really am a good father and provider. We must be doing something right if we have a daughter like this.* She opened her eyes and met Nora's smile with one of her own.

For a while, they forgot about the snow, the hens, and the lack of flour. Only love existed in their cabin.

Nora set the pot on the stove. While she waited for the water to heat so that she could scrub the wooden floor, she watched Nattie from across the room.

Her youngest was curled up in Luke's favorite armchair, a slate on her knees. She didn't know how to write yet, but she moved the piece of chalk over the slate in a fairly good imitation. With her black hair, gray-green eyes, and the frown of concentration on her little face, she looked like a two-and-a-half-year-old version of Luke.

"Where's your sister?" Nora asked. Half an hour ago, before she had gone to sweep the bedroom and wash the windows, she had left Amy with the slate to practice her ABCs. As always, Amy seemed to have lost interest quickly.

Without looking up, Nattie shrugged and mumbled, "With da horses."

It was as good a guess as any. Nora still remembered the last time Amy had disappeared. They had finally found her sleeping next to one of their draft horses.

Outside, their dog started to bark.

It wasn't the furious barking meant to chase off a coyote or an intruder. Nora smiled. She recognized the dog's greeting. Luke was home. "Hush, Bear," Nora called.

The sound of Amy's crying drowned out the barking of the dog.

Nora's smile withered. Her heart lurched into her throat. She had rarely heard such anguished cries from Amy. She pulled the pot off the stove and rushed outside.

Luke reined in her horse and dismounted, a frown on her face and a red-faced Amy in her arms.

"What happened?" Nora hurried over and ran her hands over every inch of Amy. She didn't seem hurt, but she was still sniffling.

"She climbed up on the top rail of the corral," Luke said. Her voice trembled.

Nora took one hand off Amy to squeeze Luke's arm. "Did she fall down?" It wouldn't be the first time that happened.

"No," Luke said. "She tried to climb onto one of the yearlings."

"What?" While far from being grown up, the yearlings had the unpredictable energy of adolescents and certainly weren't safe for a six-year-old to ride. "What happened?"

"She got thrown off," Luke said. "Sailed right over the corral rails." The horror of that scene was reflected in Luke's troubled gray eyes.

Once again, Nora's hands flew over her daughter's form. "Did you hurt yourself?"

Her lips pressed together, Amy shook her head.

"She's fine," Luke said, but her voice still shook. "She landed on a patch of grass. I made her move her arms and legs and looked her over before I let her stand up. There's not a scratch on her."

"Then why is she crying?"

"She's not crying because she's hurt." Luke joined Nora in brushing the grass off Amy's clothes. "She's crying because I didn't let her get back on the horse."

Nora stopped in her attempts to dry Amy's tears. She closed her eyes and shook her head. *Where on God's green earth did she get that? Certainly not from me.* Nora had always been careful around horses, even a little afraid in the beginning. When she opened her eyes again, she looked right into Luke's and had to smile. While Nattie might look like Luke, Amy was the one who had caught her horse fever. Then Nora looked at her daughter sternly. "Amy Theresa Hamilton, I know you remember what Papa keeps telling you about the horses."

Amy continued to stare at the ground.

Nora glanced at Luke, waiting for her to deliver the lesson again.

"Horses look tough, but they get scared easily," Luke said without missing a beat. "And they're really big animals, so if they run and you get in the way, you could get hurt."

"But they're my friends," Amy said, sniffling.

"Do you remember the time you bowled Nattie over when the two of you were racing to be the first to pet the puppy when we first got him?" Luke asked before Nora could think of anything to say.

Nora smiled. Two years ago, Luke would have let her handle this while she slunk away to take care of her horse. Now all awkwardness regarding the children was gone. Luke had learned to reason in a way a child could understand.

Amy nodded.

"You didn't mean to hurt your sister, did you?" Luke asked.

"No." Loud sniffles almost drowned out Amy's answer before she finally calmed down enough to talk. "But now she has a bump, like you." She pointed at Luke's nose, looking a little jealous as if that bump were a badge of honor.

"See?" Luke reached down and tapped Amy's nose. "So the horses could hurt you without even meaning to, just because they're so much bigger than you. No going off to see the horses without permission. And especially no riding. All right?"

"All right."

"Promise?" Luke held out her hand.

With a solemn expression, Amy laid her small hand into Luke's bigger one. "Promise."

They shook on it.

As soon as the handshake ended, Amy asked, "Can I go check on Measles?"

Luke exchanged a glance with Nora, then nodded. "Yes, but stay outside the stall. Don't get her riled up."

When Amy ran off to greet Measles, Nora stepped closer to say a proper hello to Luke. At the last second, she jerked back. "Eww. I thought it was Amy who reeked like that, but it's you." Instead of the comforting mix of leather, horse, and Luke, the strong smell of manure wafted up from Luke.

Luke pinched a piece of her shirt and pulled it away from her skin. "I dove out of the saddle, hoping to catch Amy. Guess I landed in something not quite sweet-smelling."

"Guess so," Nora said and kissed her anyway. "Now go change shirts, hero."

* * *

Carefully breathing through her mouth, Luke slipped off the soiled shirt. She poured water into the washbowl and wet a cloth. Habit made her hurry through her ablutions. They had taught the girls to knock before they entered the bedroom, but a lifetime of getting dressed quickly was hard to forget.

46

She strode across the room and pulled a fresh shirt from a dresser drawer.

The door swung open without warning.

"Luke!" Nora rushed into the bedroom.

Luke's heartbeat doubled. She pulled up the shirt and pressed it against her bound chest.

Nora stared at her, looking as startled as Luke felt. "Oh. Sorry."

"No, it's all right. Just ..." Luke gestured at the door, then at her state of undress. "It's an ingrained reaction. If something startles me, I just can't help it." She forced herself to move slowly as she lifted up the shirt and slipped it over her head. Nora had earned her trust, and that meant not hiding anything from her—not even her body.

Nora's gaze followed the path of the shirt as it slid down.

Over the course of the past three years, Luke had slowly gotten used to Nora studying her body, but now Nora continued to stare. "What?" Luke asked.

Nora's gaze flitted up to meet Luke's. A blush rouged her cheeks. "Sometimes, during the day, I almost forget what's under your clothes," Nora said, her voice low.

With stiff fingers, Luke jerked on the leather lacings that tied the opening of her shirt.

Two quick steps brought Nora within touching distance. Gently, she tucked the tail ends of the shirt into Luke's pants, letting her hands caress the body underneath. "It's not that I want to forget. I know most people would consider it wrong," Nora leaned forward to whisper into Luke's ear, "but I really like what's underneath your clothes."

Warm breath brushed Luke's ear, making her shiver.

She slid her hands over Nora's hips and pulled her closer.

Their lips met.

Finally, Nora pulled away, panting. "Oh!" She blinked. "You're so distracting. I came in to tell you that Measles had her foal while we were busy berating Amy for her little adventure."

"What?" Luke ran for the door, for once not bothering to put on the vest over her shirt.

As she bounded off the front porch, two hens hopped out of the way, flapping their wings, and the rooster crowed indignantly.

"I knew it." Luke had suspected that Measles would go into labor the minute she turned her back. Like many mares, Measles preferred to give birth when she was alone. Horses could stop the foaling process for days if they felt uncomfortable with being watched.

Luke bolted to the horse barn, not waiting for Nora who had stopped to pick up Nattie.

A week ago, she had put Measles into the large stall at the far end of the barn, where it was quieter. Today, curious horses poked their noses over the stall doors as Luke hurried down the center aisle.

"Papa," Amy whispered urgently. "Look!" She had long ago learned not to shout around horses, no matter how excited she was. She was clinging to the stall door with both hands, standing on her tiptoes on an overturned bucket so she could see into the stall.

Luke stopped next to her and peeked inside. Her eyes needed a moment to adjust to the dim light, but then she made out the contours of Measles, who was already back on her feet. The mare nosed through the straw, rubbing her soft lips over the foal that lay on its side.

"Look, Papa. The foal got red hair, just like me." Amy

fidgeted on the bucket, almost knocking it over.

Luke heaved her up, into her arms. The girl was getting too big to be held like this for much longer. "I see it," she said, not as enthusiastic. While the sorrel coat was nice, she'd hoped for a multicolored foal. Measles's first foal didn't have any spots as far as Luke could see.

Measles nickered softly to her foal and pushed at its rear end with her nose.

Its long, thin legs splayed and trembling, the foal stood.

Luke grinned.

A small white blanket, littered with reddish dots, covered the foal's hind end.

Nora stepped up next to her, balancing Nattie on one hip. Now four pairs of eyes were watching the newborn foal stagger through the stall until it found its mother's teats and began to suckle. "Oh, how beautiful," Nora whispered. "A multicolored foal—just like you hoped for."

Luke's heart sang. She wrapped her free arm around Nora and pulled her close against her side. Could life get any better?

"Papa," Amy's voice broke the comfortable silence. "Can the foal be my horse? I can teach her to be a good horse, like Measles."

Luke nearly choked on her own spit, almost making her drop the girl. "Um." She looked at Nora.

Nora stared back. "Sweetie, you're just six years old. You're too small to take care of a horse, much less train a foal."

Tears glittered in Amy's pleading green eyes.

This was the one thing Luke still hadn't learned: how to face tears from one of her daughters. "You can help me with the foal," she said. "And if you do a really good job, in a few years, when the foal is grown up and has her own foal, that'll be yours and you can train her. All right?"

Their neighbors would talk and shake their heads at Luke for letting a girl train a young horse, but Luke didn't care. She had promised herself that their daughters would be allowed to do whatever they wanted.

Amy threw her arms around Luke's neck in a strangle hold.

"Luke Hamilton! That girl has you wrapped around her little finger," Nora said, but her voice sounded affectionate, not really scolding. She glanced down at Nattie. "Both of them do."

Luke leaned over and kissed her cheek. "All three of them."

"Papa?" Nattie tugged on Luke's sleeve.

"Yes, little one?"

"I want baby," Nattie said.

Nora's groan made Luke chuckle. "You want a baby horse too?"

Nattie shook her head.

"Then what?" For Luke, it was often easier to understand Amy's needs and interests than those of her younger daughter. Never before had she seen two siblings more different than these two.

Amy rolled her eyes. "She wants a baby sister because I don't want to play with her."

Heat shot up Luke's neck and suffused her cheeks. She rubbed the bridge of her nose and shot Nora a helpless glance.

Now Nora, equally red-faced, was the one who chuckled. "That's what you get for spoiling them. Try to talk your way out of this one."

"Thanks so much," Luke mumbled. She looked into

Nattie's gray-green eyes, which were watching her expectantly. "Um, how about a kitten?"

Nora laughed so loudly that even Measles looked up from her nursing foal.

"Sssh, Mama!" Amy poked her in the shoulder. "No loud noises around the horses."

"Yes, Mama," Nattie said, quite seriously. Thankfully, she seemed to have forgotten all about her wish for a baby sister—at least for now.

Phew. Luke wiped her brow. A child was the one thing she could never give her family, no matter how hard she worked.

"Hey," Nora whispered into her ear. "Don't look so glum. You think either of us could survive a third little one like this? Let's try raising these two without going crazy, all right?"

She's right. Luke turned, touched her lips to Nora's, and said, "I'll give it my best."

###

THE ART OF PRETENDING

Independence, Missouri
September 12th, 1856

What a pity. Frankie Callaghan glanced at the cards in her hand again. Ten of hearts. Jack of hearts. Queen of hearts. King of hearts. If she drew the ace, she'd have a chance at a royal flush. *I haven't had a hand that good in, well, forever.* She suppressed a sigh and threw down her cards. "I fold," she said to the men playing poker with her.

The gray-bearded man to her right clapped her on the shoulder. "Maybe you'd have better luck at the faro table, young man."

Luck is not the problem. Frankie wasn't here to win. Winning the pot with a royal flush would draw attention, and that was the last thing she needed. At least folding gave her a chance to lean back and look around while the poker game kept the men around her busy.

She glanced toward the mahogany bar and the man who was responsible for Frankie's visit to Independence. Jeffrey Donovan was deeply in conversation with a golden-haired beauty. It wasn't hard to guess that she was Tess Swenson, the brothel's madam. She was older than the other women in the room, and the quiet confidence in her gaze told Frankie that she was a woman used to being in a position of responsibility.

Tess Swenson stood and adjusted the low-cut bodice revealing a still firm body. She gave Jeff Donovan a nod and pointed at the stairs. To anyone watching, she would look like a prostitute inviting a customer up to her room.

Frankie wasn't just anyone, though. Her trained eye noticed that Tess's gestures were neither seductive nor submissive; they had the resoluteness of a commanding officer. Tess was practically ordering Donovan up to her room.

He's not just a customer to her. They know each other in more than the biblical sense.

Tess trailed after the man. When she reached the bottom of the stairs, she turned back around. Her vigilant gaze swept the room, making sure everything was all right with her girls.

Frankie quickly looked away, not wanting to be noticed. She chugged down her lukewarm beer, hiding behind the glass until Tess had turned back around.

The old man next to her grinned at Frankie. "You had your eye on her, huh? No luck on that front either, young man."

Frankie would be keeping an eye on Tess Swenson, but not for the reason the old man was thinking.

* * *

"Vanish?" Tess repeated. She stared at her business partner through narrowed eyes. "How can five thousand dollar just vanish—for the second time this month?"

Jeff Donovan shrugged. "Every cent of the money was there when we sealed the box, but when the stagecoach arrived in Salt Lake City, the money was gone."

Tess had understood that the first time he had said it, but she bit her tongue and curbed her impatience. She couldn't afford to antagonize Donovan. His name was on each of the businesses Tess owned, except for the brothel. He didn't provide even half the money or the business acumen in their partnership, but Tess hadn't chosen him for that. She had enough money and business sense on her own, but no one in town would do business with a woman, much less with the madam of the brothel. To the world, Jeffrey Donovan was the sole owner of a stable, a boarding house, the best restaurant, and the biggest saloon in Independence, while Tess pulled the strings behind the scenes.

"Any idea what happened to the money?" Tess asked, fighting to stay calm.

"There's a lot of things that could have gone wrong between Independence and Salt Lake City," Donovan said. "Twenty days is a long time."

Sending the money by stagecoach wasn't exactly safe. Tess knew that. Sometimes boxes got lost, but twice in a row was more than just a coincidence. "Did you send an armed guard to accompany the stagecoach like I told you to?"

"I even sent two, but it was of no use. By the time the stagecoach reached Salt Lake City, the money was gone."

"What about the stage driver and the people running the stage stations along the way?" Tess asked. "Do you trust them?"

Donovan ran his hand through his thinning hair. "I don't know them well enough to trust or distrust them." He looked at her like a soldier awaiting his commander's orders.

What now? Tess silently considered her options.

Turning to the sheriff for help was not one of them. The brothel was a thorn in the sheriff's side already. If he took a closer look at her businesses, he would discover that Donovan wasn't the sole owner. Tess couldn't risk that. "I'll think of something," she said. "Until further notice, don't send off any more money or goods."

Donovan nodded. He slipped out of his coat and started to undo the buttons of his pants.

"No." Tess picked up the coat and handed it back to Donovan. "Not today, Jeffrey." She had shared her bed with Donovan before—not because she found him desirable in any way, but simply as a means to ensure his loyalty. Today, she just didn't have the time or the patience to humor him.

Donovan clenched his jaw and jerked his coat back on.

"It's better if you aren't seen spending too much time with me anyway," Tess said, trying to placate him. "We wouldn't want the sheriff—or your wife—to find out about our association."

"Right," Donovan said.

Tess stepped closer and straightened the collar of his coat for him, letting her hand trail over his chest for a moment. "We'll have our own little celebration as soon as we find the money." *Nothing like giving him a bit of an incentive.* She hid a grin.

Donovan licked his lips and finally retreated from the room.

Independence, Missouri
September 13th, 1856

"That's a lovely color, Frances," Sara Donovan said, leaning over the table to take a closer look at the work in Frankie's embroidery hoop.

Frankie finished the center of one tiny flower with a French knot and paused, the needle resting securely between her index finger and thumb. "My late husband brought back the embroidery silk from his last business trip. He loved to surprise me with little gifts," she said with a grave expression. Frankie had never been married, nor had she ever received gifts from men, but the three women in Mrs. Donovan's parlor didn't know that.

Mrs. Donovan laid down her knitting needles to pat Frankie's hand.

"I wish my husband were more like that," one of Mrs. Donovan's friends murmured. "He never brings me back anything when he's away on business."

The two other women nodded.

"Never?" Frankie looked from woman to woman, finally resting her gaze on Mrs. Donovan. She wasn't interested in the answers of the other two women.

"Well, Jeffrey brought back a new apron from Salt Lake City once," Mrs. Donovan answered.

Now it's getting interesting. Frankie daintily sipped her tea, hiding her acute interest. "Does your husband have to travel to Salt Lake City a lot?"

"No." Mrs. Donovan shook her head. "He's hardly had to travel at all in the last few years."

Frankie looked up from the tiny, olive green leaf she was stitching. "I hope that doesn't mean his business is not going well?"

"Oh, no, not at all." Mrs. Donovan proudly lifted her head. "As far as I can tell, business is going just fine."

As far as I can tell. Frankie suppressed the urge to grimace. Befriending Sara Donovan had been a waste of time. *As long as there's enough money for her to spend, she doesn't care where it comes from. I bet she has never asked her husband about the details of his job.* She stared down at the embroidered linen without really seeing it. *So if Donovan's wife is clueless, maybe I should take a closer look at his mistress. The question is just how.*

For once, being a woman had her at a disadvantage. With other assignments, it had mostly worked in her favor, giving her options her male colleagues didn't have. And if her female charms reached their limits, she could always become Frank Callaghan. She was as convincing in the role of the young man as she was playing the rich widow. But slipping into male disguise wouldn't be enough this time. Getting close to a prostitute to find out more about her would inevitably mean sharing her bed. *And as pleasurable as that would be, Frankie, it would surely blow your cover.* She stared at the needle in her hand, trying to come up with a plan.

Independence, Missouri
September 14th, 1856

Tess wrapped her shawl more tightly around her shoulders and held her head high, ignoring the glances of the townspeople who were on their way home from church. *Hypocrites.* The men who were now ignoring her and who had eagerly nodded to the preacher's sermon against sin and sinners would just as eagerly try to share her bed tonight.

Over the years, Tess had grown used to it and had learned not to react, but deep down, being constantly slighted hurt nonetheless. She walked on, rounding the corner on her way to the stage driver's home. By tomorrow, the stage driver would be on his way to Salt Lake City again, and Tess had a few questions that brooked no delay.

Only her quick reflexes prevented her from colliding head-on with Sara Donovan and three of her friends.

Mrs. Donovan grazed her with a contemptuous gaze and mumbled something Tess didn't even want to understand. Two of the younger women in Mrs. Donovan's entourage put their heads together and started to whisper, no doubt sharing the latest gossip about Tess. Then, like all the other proper townswomen, they quickly crossed to the other side of the road.

Tess's gaze followed them. She looked at Mrs. Donovan, one of her fiercest enemies in town. *I wonder how you would react if you knew how familiar I am with your husband. Or maybe you already know, and that's why you hate me so much.*

Just as Tess wanted to continue on her way, Mrs. Donovan's newest friend, a brown-haired, slender, and altogether ordinary woman, turned.

Tess straightened her shoulders, preparing for another hostile glare.

Instead, the stranger looked at her with compassion, respect, and just the hint of a smile.

Tess blinked. When she opened her eyes again, the woman had turned back around and was hastily catching up with her friends.

For a second, Tess was almost convinced that moment of contact had never happened, but she could still feel the woman's gaze resting on her, brief as that glance had been. No one had looked at her like that in a long time. *Five years,* her precise mind supplied, and a mental picture of Luke and Nora formed in her mind's eye. *Hope you're well, my friends.* While she was glad that Nora had managed to leave the brothel and start a new life with Luke, she sometimes missed them.

But Tess wasn't one to dwell on the past and on things she couldn't have, so she forced her thoughts back to the present and to Mrs. Donovan's new friend. The woman was probably new in town and didn't know who—and what—Tess was. *Next time you'll meet her, she won't look at you the same way—if she'll look at you at all. Mrs. Donovan will waste no time informing her about your depravity.* Tess lifted her chin. *Well, it's not like you need her approval. You've got better things to do than worry about what people think.*

Straightening her dress with one hand, Tess knocked on the stage driver's door.

* * *

Later that night, Tess made her way down the brothel's hallway, stopping in front of every door to listen for a moment. Grunts and moans came from behind Molly's door, and someone was snoring in Rose's room. Satisfied that her girls were all right, Tess continued on her way to her office.

It had been a quiet evening, so Tess had retreated much earlier than usual. Feeling restless, she had decided to head upstairs and write a letter to Nora and Luke, something she often did when she needed to talk to someone she could trust.

She opened the door to her office and waited until her eyes had adjusted to the darkness before she crossed the room to light the kerosene lamp on her desk. After groping around for a few seconds, she found the matches and lifted the glass chimney.

A sudden sound stopped her from lighting the match.

Tess paused and listened in the darkness.

There it was again. A scraping sound came from just below the office's window.

Tess had lived a dangerous life, and she had learned to be cautious. A prostitute didn't reach the ripe old age of thirty-six by being careless. Quickly, she let go of the chimney and ducked down behind her desk.

Everything was quiet; only the sound of her own breathing echoed loudly in Tess's ears. *Guess I'm imagining things.*

She was about to get up from behind her hiding place when the scraping sound came again.

Tess froze and held her breath.

Metal scratched over wood. Slowly, the office's small window was forced open.

Tess pressed herself against the desk. Her hand shot down and reached for the Philadelphia Deringer hidden in one of her garters.

Boots thumped on the floor as an intruder slipped through the window and landed just a yard away from her.

Tess didn't give him time to orient himself. She had to take advantage of the few seconds his eyes needed to adjust to the darkness in the office. She jumped out from behind the desk and cocked her weapon's hammer.

A loud click reverberated through the office.

The intruder stood stock-still.

"I don't know who you are, thief, but if you move a muscle, you'll be dead," Tess said. Her voice was as hard and unyielding as the barrel she pressed against the intruder's side.

Slowly, the intruder lifted his hands, showing Tess that he was unarmed. He didn't speak, and his back prevented the moonlight from falling into the office, so Tess had no idea who he was.

"Light the lamp so I can see your face," Tess said. She nodded toward the kerosene lamp on the desk. "Slow movements."

The intruder's hands didn't tremble as he lit the lamp and turned up the wick.

The flickering light revealed a stranger's face. If Tess had ever seen him before, she didn't remember. She wouldn't blame herself. There was nothing memorable about the man. Everything about him was average: his height, his build, his clothes, and even the brown hair sticking out from under his unremarkable hat. "Who are you?" Tess encouraged an answer by waving the Deringer at him.

"I'm not a thief," the intruder said. Even his voice was average, neither deep nor high-pitched.

"Oh, really? You could have fooled me." For some

reason, Tess didn't feel threatened by the intruder, but she kept on her guard nonetheless. "For someone who is not a thief, you are awfully good at scaling balconies and breaking into houses."

The intruder gave a nod as if Tess had just paid him a compliment. "Thank you," he said, humor coloring his voice. "This is the first time I ever got caught. You're awfully good too."

"That's what all the visitors who come up here say," Tess answered. "Most of them have the decency to come through the door, though." She lifted the Deringer a little, now aiming right between his eyes. "Who are you, and what do you want?"

No answer came.

"If you don't want to answer me, maybe you'll be more talkative with the sheriff," Tess said.

The stranger smiled as if he knew she wouldn't call the sheriff.

Getting impatient, Tess took a quick step forward and knocked the hat from his head with her free hand, revealing more of his face. *I know this face!* Never forgetting a face was part of what had ensured Tess's survival all these years. She tried to remember where she had seen him before. *Wasn't he one of the men playing poker with the doc earlier this week?*

Tess stepped closer to study him, careful not to give him any chance to take the weapon from her. She shoved the muzzle under his chin, forcing him to lift his head and look at her.

Their gazes met.

Tess gasped and took a step back. "It's you!" The brown eyes might have been unremarkable when it came to their color, but something in the stranger's gaze was anything but average. Tess identified it immediately, even when her logical mind told her it was impossible. *This is the woman who was out for a walk with Mrs. Donovan.*

The mysterious stranger shifted from foot to foot. Tess's exclamation and her wide-eyed gaze had managed what the Deringer couldn't: making him—or her—nervous. "What do you mean?"

"I saw you," Tess said.

The stranger shrugged. "All right. Yes, I've visited your establishment before. I played poker with a few—"

"No." Tess slashed her hand through the air. "I saw you with Sara Donovan. You were wearing a dress."

"Oh, you mean Frances, my twin sister." The stranger laughed, but to Tess's trained ear, it sounded fake and nervous.

Tess hesitated. *It's the most logical explanation.* Still, it didn't feel right. *A twin sister might have the same height, the same hair, and the same brown eyes, but she wouldn't look at me with the exact same expression. No.* She shook her head. These were the eyes that had looked at her with respect while Sara Donovan had thrown contemptuous glances her way. "You can't fool me," she said. "I've met others like you."

"Others like me?" The stranger tilted his—or her—head.

"Women who prefer living their lives in male disguise," Tess said.

The stranger stared at her. "I don't know what you're talking about. I'm not a woman. That's ridiculous."

"Is it?" Tess stepped closer, careful to keep the pistol trained on the stranger.

"Yeah, it's completely—"

Tess didn't listen. Her free hand shot up and pressed

against the stranger's chest.

With a sound of surprise, the stranger tried to jump back and escape Tess's hand, but Tess was too fast.

Tess's dexterous fingers slipped beneath the jacket. "Well, this is definitely the finest breast I've ever felt on a man," she said, a little out of breath from their struggle. She gently squeezed the bound breast beneath the shirt.

The stranger froze, her chest heaving under Tess's hand.

"Tess?" Molly's voice came from the hallway. Her steps came closer. "That bastard Billy refuses to pay and—"

Tess half-turned and shouted, "Stay back!" She didn't want one of her girls to get involved in a potentially dangerous situation. "I'll be there in a—"

Strong hands shoved Tess back.

Refusing to let go of the weapon, Tess couldn't break her fall with the hand closest to the desk. Her hip collided with the edge of the desk. Pain shot through her. Gritting her teeth, Tess whirled around, pistol at the ready to face another attack.

It never came.

The place where the stranger had stood was empty.

"Dammit!" Tess rushed to the still open window.

A drunken customer staggered down the street, but the mysterious stranger was nowhere to be seen.

"Tess?" Molly called again. "Everythin' all right?"

Tess sighed. *No.* Nothing in her life seemed to be all right anymore. Someone was stealing her money, and now this strange woman had broken into her office. Tess closed the window and stepped into the hallway. "Everything's fine, Mol."

Donovan's Boarding House
Independence, Missouri
September 15th, 1856

Tess peered through the partially open stable door. Her eyes burned, and she suppressed a yawn. By Tess's standards, it was still early in the day. After a late night settling disputes between her girls and the customers, she had dragged her tired body out of bed to keep an eye on the boarding house across the street.

The door of the boarding house had opened a few times and lodgers had stepped out, but it was never the woman who had broken into Tess's office last night.

Tess knew the boarding house was where she was staying, though. It wasn't hard to find out when you were the boarding house's owner and had access to the establishment's books. A week ago, a young gentleman had signed in as "Frank Callaghan." According to the porter, the young man was traveling with his sister, a wealthy widow.

"Wealthy widow," Tess murmured. "I bet her wealth and her late husband are as fake as everything else about her."

The boarding house's door opened once more, and her mysterious burglar stepped out, taking a second to adjust her hat. To the world, she was the perfect gentleman.

She's good. There was nothing feminine about the way the stranger moved. Her stride and her gestures were confident, as if she had spent a lot of time in male apparel and was entirely comfortable in her disguise.

Tess waited until the woman who called herself Frank Callaghan had disappeared down the street, then she quickly crossed the street and slipped into the boarding house. A few words to the porter, one of very few people who knew where his wages really came from, and she had the master key that would open the door to Frank Callaghan's room.

Callaghan had picked the out-of-the-way room at the end of the hall.

Tess let herself in, closed the door behind her, and looked around.

The bed was already made, and the room was kept tidy and clean. There were no personal belongings, nothing that gave away whether it was a man or a woman who had rented this room.

Tess looked under the bed and rummaged through drawers. Two dresses hung in the closet, side by side with a man's suit. Tess let her hand trail along the jacket, recognizing it as the one her intruder had worn the night before. She furrowed her brow when she felt the contours of something in the jacket. "What's this?" She slipped her fingers into the jacket's inside pocket.

It was a small notebook. Its owner had apparently forgotten to transfer it to the jacket she was wearing now.

Tess opened the notebook. On the very first page, she found detailed information about the stage line transporting money and goods between Salt Lake City and Independence. All the departure times, the stations along the way, and the names of the stage drivers were written down in clear, bold letters.

"I knew it!" Tess waved the little book in the air. She had known it couldn't be just a coincidence—the strange woman had befriended Sara Donovan, had rented a room in Donovan's boarding house, and had broken into Tess's office. *She's the one who is stealing my money! Now the question is, is she working alone. And what is she planning next?*

Tess turned the page. The information on the next page made it obvious that the stranger had watched Jeff Donovan for quite some time. She had written down details on his house, his wife, and his daily routine, including where he preferred to eat, when he left the house each morning, and how he spent his lunch break.

Tess flipped through the pages—and then stopped. Right there, in the middle of the little book, were the intimate details of her life. One page listed the names of the men she had led upstairs to her room in the past week. The time when she retreated each night had been meticulously noted. "Frank" Callaghan had even noticed that, while Tess plied her customers with drinks at the bar, her own glass held only cold tea that looked like whiskey.

On the next page, a pencil drawing of her face looked back at Tess. The detailed description underneath it sounded like a "wanted" poster—except for one word written at the bottom of the page, as if it had only been added reluctantly: beautiful.

Frowning, not sure what to think of all this, Tess slipped the notebook back into the jacket pocket and continued to look around. In the back of the closet, she found a hidden bag. When Tess opened it, she found half a dozen hairpieces in different colors, rouge, a pair of glasses, a fake mustache, and a number of scarves, hats, and other accessories. It looked like the bag of a play-actor—or a con man.

The sudden sound of a key turning in the lock interrupted Tess.

Damn. Tess slammed the closet door shut and looked around for some place to hide, but it was already too late.

The door swung open, revealing the woman who

called herself Frank Callaghan. She stood frozen in the doorway for a moment. "So we meet again." She drew her revolver and pointed it at Tess almost casually. Even as she took off her hat and gave a little bow, the weapon in her hand never wavered. "You are certainly persistent and resourceful. I have to give you that." She kicked the door closed, took a step closer, and looked down at Tess from a height advantage of just a few inches. Despite the revolver in her hand, the gaze that rested on Tess was not threatening, just curious.

Tess curled her hands into fists. *She might have a few things in common with Luke, but don't let that delude you into thinking you can trust her.*

"Now it's my turn to ask: What are you doing here?" the stranger asked.

Tess raised her chin. "Believe it or not, but once upon a time I was taught how to be a lady. My mother told me that a lady always has to pay a return visit."

The woman laughed. "You're amusing, if not honest. How did you get in here?"

A knock at the door interrupted whatever answer Tess might have given. "Mister Callaghan?" Sara Donovan's voice came through the door.

"Damn," Frank Callaghan muttered.

Tess looked back and forth between the woman and the window. Should she take the opportunity and escape through the window, as Callaghan had the night before? But she wasn't sure if she could safely make it down to the street, and if anybody saw her climbing down and called the sheriff, he would arrest her with pleasure.

Sara Donovan knocked on the door again. "Mister Callaghan, are you there?"

"Um, yes," Ms. Callaghan answered, lowering her

voice.

"I couldn't find your sister, so I thought I would come over and tell you the good news myself," Mrs. Donovan called through the door. "My husband agreed to give you the job."

Looks like all her secret observations finally paid off. She tricked the Donovans into trusting her, but now that she knows it won't work with me, she'll try to get rid of me. Tess realized she had to act quickly. She rushed across the room and threw open the door before the surprised woman could stop her, hoping Ms. Callaghan wouldn't shoot her in front of witnesses. Calmly, she greeted Mrs. Donovan, who stood frozen in front of the door and stared at her.

"You had that ... that woman in your room?" Sara Donovan stammered.

"It's not what you think," Ms. Callaghan said.

Tess snickered. *Oh, yeah, that excuse worked so well for every man who got caught with a lady of the evening.* She strode past Mrs. Donovan and hurried down the stairs.

The last thing Tess heard was Mrs. Donovan's appalled, "Oh, what your poor sister is going to say when she hears about this."

Frankie tied down the last piece of baggage on top of the stagecoach. As she climbed down, she threw a furtive glance at the treasure box the stage driver was stowing under his seat. Judging from the way he struggled with the box's weight, it had to contain a lot of money, gold, and other objects of value.

"So, you're the new shotgun messenger?" the stage driver asked when Frankie took her seat next to him. "Can you handle these?" He pointed at the revolver at Frankie's hip and the shotgun she held in the bend of her arm.

Frankie flashed a confident grin. She had grown up with five brothers and could handle a weapon better than any one of them. "Can you handle these?" she asked, nodding down at the lines resting in the driver's callused hands.

The driver looked affronted for a moment but then laughed. "Just wait until all the passengers have climbed in. Then I'll show you how I handle the lines."

Frankie nodded and watched as an overweight businessman, an old woman and her son, and finally one of Mrs. Donovan's friends with her baby arrived and took their seats inside the stagecoach.

Still, the stage driver held back the four horses. "We're still one passenger short," he said at Frankie's questioning gaze.

A woman hurried toward them, her long skirt clutched in one hand, pulling it up just a bit so she wouldn't stumble. When she stopped next to the driver's seat and handed the ticket to the driver, Frankie did a double take.

Tess Swenson. Now that she was dressed in a respectable

long skirt and a chaste bodice and had her gold-blond hair pinned up under a bonnet, Frankie almost hadn't recognized the woman. For a moment, she was worried that Tess would tell the other travelers that Frankie was a woman, but then she inwardly shook her head. If Tess had wanted to do that, she would have done it after Frankie had broken into her office. *She's got something to hide, and she doesn't want to draw attention.*

Tess stared at Frankie. Her lips compressed into a thin line.

Am I spoiling your plans to steal even more money? Frankie climbed back down to help Tess into the stagecoach.

"What are you planning?" Tess whispered.

Frankie touched her chest in a gesture of innocence. "Me? What are you planning?" She opened the stagecoach's door for Tess.

"Oh, no," one of the ladies already inside cried. "I'm not traveling with the likes of her."

"I bought a ticket just like everyone else," Tess said. She stood in front of the stagecoach, holding her head up with, even under the other woman's contemptuous gaze.

Frankie couldn't help admiring her.

"I'm not sharing a seat with a ... a whore!" Mrs. Donovan's friend blocked the door.

"Make up your minds, ladies," the driver called. "I'll leave on time, with or without you."

Frankie made a quick decision. "You can have my seat." She pointed at the seat next to the driver. It was the best seat on the stagecoach anyway. The upholstered seats inside might look more comfortable, but the driver's seat was subjected to fewer bumps and jars. "I'll make myself comfortable on the roof."

Tess stared at her with a stunned expression. Her piercing gaze searched for an ulterior motive.

What the hell are you doing? Frankie silently asked herself. *You should have taken the opportunity to make sure she was left behind in Independence.* "The view is much better from up there anyway. Will make it easier to keep an eye on stagecoach robbers," she said, looking right at Tess. She extended her hand and politely helped Tess to climb up on the seat next to the driver. She held a pleasant smile on her lips, even as Tess and she stared daggers at each other.

During the next few hours, Frankie had ample opportunity to observe Tess as the stagecoach rattled along the dusty road.

If Tess sensed her gaze, she didn't let it show. She never turned around; she just sat with her head held high, never once complaining about the dust, the constant jostling, or the uncomfortable seat.

What a strange woman, Frankie thought, intrigued against her will. No one had ever discovered her true identity, and Frankie still didn't know how Tess had seen through her disguise so easily. *What was it that gave me away?*

She still didn't have an answer when they reached the station where they would stay the night.

Mrs. Donovan's friend complained loudly about the crude adobe structures and the simple supper of beans, bread, and salt pork, but once again, Tess never said a word.

The station keeper came over to the table to refill their tin cups with bad coffee. "I don't have enough rooms for all of you," he said. "The ladies will have to share a room."

"What?" Mrs. Donovan's friend jumped up from the table. "How dare you suggest I share a room with that ... with that woman?" She glared at the station keeper, then at Tess.

Once again, Frankie found herself coming to Tess's rescue before she could stop herself. "You can have my room," she said to Tess. "I'll sleep in the stable and keep an eye on the freight." She told herself it was a clever plan to stay close to the treasure box and its valuable contents, but she had made her offer before she had even thought about that. Tess might be the manipulative, cunning, and possibly dishonest madam of a brothel, but Frankie didn't like to see her treated like this anyway.

"That's not necessary," Tess said. "I will sleep in the stable."

Frankie suppressed a snort. *Like I'd leave you alone with the treasure box.* "No," she said. "Take the room. I'm used to sleeping in the stable."

Tess opened her mouth, no doubt about to object again.

"Let the young man be a gentleman," the station keeper said. "He's getting paid for this, after all."

Tess didn't look pleased, but she finally nodded. "Thank you," she said, but the cool gaze she directed at Frankie said something else.

Frankie had to hide a grin. "You're welcome."

Frankie crossed her arms behind her head and stared into the darkness.

The straw to her left rustled.

She rolled out from under her blanket, drawing her revolver.

Hooves scraped over the ground.

Frankie shoved her revolver back into the holster. *Just one of the horses, searching for a midnight snack.* Instead of slipping under her blanket again, she lit a lantern and hung it on a peg. Yawning, she made her way to the back of the stable, where the treasure box and other pieces of baggage were stored. She knelt down next to the wooden box and trailed her hand over its surface, testing the sturdiness of the lock.

The rustling of straw next to her warned her at the very last moment.

Frankie whirled around.

The barrel of a weapon that had been aimed at her head only hit her in the shoulder, paralyzing her arm for a moment.

Her weapon clattered to the floor.

Frankie gripped her attacker's arm and felt her attacker grab her in return. With both hands out of commission, Frankie swept at her attacker's legs with a powerful kick.

Both of them landed in the straw, tussling for the weapon.

Frankie couldn't see her attacker's face, but at this close range, with their bodies pressed against each other as they wrestled to get a grip on the pistol, she knew she was fighting with a woman. "Give up, Tess!"

"And let you have the money? Never!" Tess said, sounding as breathless as Frankie.

The pain in Frankie's shoulder finally lessened, and she managed to get a hold of Tess's wrists. She pressed them over Tess's head and into the straw, shackling them to the ground with her own hands. "Give up!" She held Tess down with her weight.

Tess bucked and writhed under her, trying to get free.

"You're only wasting your time." Frankie held Tess's wrists in a secure grip. No way in hell would Tess get free. Growing up with five wild brothers had taught Frankie all the tricks.

Tess didn't give up, though. She threw her body weight against Frankie in an attempt to throw her off. Her breasts pressed into Frankie's, and a tendril of blond hair teased Frankie's cheek. Then Tess's mouth was on her own.

Frankie lost her grip on Tess's wrists as she got lost in the warmth of those lips. *Stop!* Frankie shouted herself after several intoxicating moments. *Stop it. This is not professional.* Slowly, reluctantly, she broke the kiss—but it was already too late.

Something pressed against her side, and the resounding click of a hammer being pulled back told her it was not just Tess's finger.

Frankie clenched her hands to helpless fists. *Dumb, dumb, dumb! Your brothers never taught you that little trick. You should have seen this coming. You've observed her long enough to know how she operates. She's working in a brothel, for heaven's sake, so you couldn't seriously think that kiss was anything but an attempt to distract you.*

"Get off me," Tess said.

Gritting her teeth, Frankie rolled to the side.

Tess quickly got to her feet. With the Deringer still pointing at Frankie, she took the lantern from its peg and made her way over to the treasure box.

Frankie searched around in the straw for her revolver, which she had dropped earlier, but came up empty.

Tess knelt down next to the wooden box and set down the lantern, one eye and the Deringer's barrel still on Frankie.

This is where it gets difficult. The box was too heavy for Tess to carry it off on her own, and if she shot at the lock, she would wake up everyone in the house.

Tess reached into her dress, her fingers trailing down her breasts.

Frankie's pulse quickened. *What is she doing?*

Tess's hand reappeared. The lantern's light glinted on something in Tess's palm. For a moment, Tess fumbled with the lock, then the lid of the wooden box swung open.

Frankie stared at her. *Jesus.* Somehow, Tess had gotten her hands on the key, which should have been safe somewhere in Independence and Salt Lake City. *She's even more resourceful than I thought.*

Then Tess whirled around and rushed toward Frankie. She grabbed the collar of Frankie's shirt with one hand and shoved the pistol up under her chin with the other. Almost nose to nose with Frankie, she glared at her. "Where is it?"

Frankie stared into Tess's blue eyes that seemed gray in the semi-darkness of the stable. "W-what?"

"Where—" Tess pressed the Deringer's muzzle more tightly against Frankie's skin.

"—is—"

The pressure increased.

"—my—"

The cold steel forced Frankie to sink into the straw.

"—money?" Tess glared down at Frankie, kneeling over her like an avenging angel.

Frankie swallowed, not sure whether it was the pressure of the weapon against her throat or the fire in Tess's eyes that was making her breathless. "Your money?"

"Don't play dumb!" Tess leaned over her, her knee pressing against Frankie's crotch. "How did you get your hands on the money without damaging the lock?"

Frankie squirmed against the pressure of Tess's knee. She was struggling to gather her thoughts and make sense of what was happening. "Wait! Wait a moment." She gasped. "I don't have the money. I thought you—"

"Does this look like I have it?" Tess finally moved away just enough for Frankie to get a glance at the overturned treasure box.

It was empty.

"Where is my money?" Tess asked again.

Frankie shook her head. "Do you think I would still be here if I had stolen the money? I would have taken one of the horses and would be miles away by now."

"Looks like your nice little plan didn't work, huh?"

"Looks like yours didn't work either," Frankie said. "All that work to get your hands on the key has been for nothing. Seems like a cleverer thief was faster than you."

Tess stared at her. "Cleverer thief? Are you implying that I'm a thief too?"

Frankie smiled grimly. "Why else would you be here in the middle of the night? As nice as that kiss was, you certainly didn't come over to kiss me goodnight."

"I came to make sure you didn't ride off with my money," Tess answered, her voice raised.

"Your money?" Tess had said it a few times now. "The

box was full to overflowing. How can all of it be your money?" The brothel might be lucrative, but it certainly didn't make enough money to fill the treasure box. The girls in Tess's establishment were better fed and clothed than in most other brothels Frankie had seen, so not all the money went into Tess's pocket.

"It's the money I earned with my stable, my restaurant, my brothel, and my saloon—and thank you very much for your contribution, which you made by staying in my boarding house." Tess smirked.

Frankie shook her head. "You're lying," she said, not even blinking when the pistol was pointed at her head again. "I've seen the records in the land office. Jeffrey Donovan is the sole owner of the boarding house, the restaurant, and everything else. The money is his."

"Donovan owns everything on paper only," Tess said. "The only thing he contributes to our business relationship is his name and his reputation as an honest businessman. I'm the one with the money."

Frankie let her head sink back into the straw. She had been taught not to trust suspects, but she believed Tess. "Looks like he's not so honest after all."

"What?" Tess frowned.

"Jeffrey Donovan," Frankie said. "Looks like he's not as honest as you thought."

Tess narrowed her eyes. "Oh, now you're accusing him?"

"Well, whoever stole the money must have a key to the treasure box. He or she made good use of it before we even left Independence," Frankie said. "One person comes to mind."

"Yes." Tess growled. "You! You spied on Donovan and me for weeks. You broke into my office. You manipulated

Donovan into giving you a job as a shotgun messenger. You disguised yourself, and all because—"

"All because," Frankie said, "I'm a Pinkerton detective, hired by the stage line. Donovan asked them to find the thief and return his stolen money, or he'll hold them liable."

For a few moments, they stared at each other in silence.

Then Tess laughed. "Oh, yes, of course. Female Pinkerton detectives. There are hundreds of them."

"Not hundreds, but there are a few," Frankie said. "Just like there are a few women who own saloons, restaurants, boarding houses, and stables."

Tess slowly lowered her weapon but kept it pointing in Frankie's general direction. She tilted her head. "I've never heard of a female Pinkerton detective."

"Neither has Jeffrey Donovan—and that's my advantage," Frankie said. "Men like him don't see me as a threat, so they're not very careful about what they reveal in my presence."

"So what did Donovan reveal?" Tess asked. She kept her face expressionless, not revealing whether she believed Frankie.

Frankie shrugged. "Not much. I should have pursued that lead more insistently, but I got distracted."

"Distracted?"

"I thought you had stolen the money," Frankie said.

Tess snorted. "Oh, yeah, I'm a whore, so of course I have to be a thief, too."

"It has nothing to do with you being ... with what you do for a living," Frankie said, meaning it. She got up on her knees and looked Tess in the eyes. "It was just the most plausible explanation. You're ... friends with Jeff Donovan, so I thought he might have told you about the money in a ... weak moment. You asked around for details about the stage line, and instead of calling the sheriff on me after I broke into your office, you broke into my room. Now tell me you wouldn't find that suspicious."

Tess was silent for a moment. "I guess it could seem a little suspicious," she finally said. She studied Frankie closely. "What proof do I have that you're really a Pinkerton and not just out to trick me and get your hands on my money?"

Frankie fished in the inside pocket of her vest.

"Stop!" Tess's weapon swung up, pointing at Frankie again.

Frankie held out her other hand in a placatory gesture. "I just want to show you my credentials." Slowly, she pulled the brass badge out of her pocket and held it out for Tess to see.

Still pointing the Deringer at Frankie, Tess stepped closer and took the badge. With her fingertips, she traced the engraved letters, which formed the words "Pinkerton National Detective Agency." Finally, she looked up at Frankie. "So you really are a lady detective?"

Frankie grinned. "Well, I'm a detective—the lady part is debatable."

Tess stared at her, then chuckled. "I've never met anyone like you before," she said with a shake of her head.

"No?" Frankie quirked an eyebrow. "I thought you said you'd met others like me?"

"I was wrong about that," Tess murmured.

Is that a good or a bad thing?

Tess slid up her dress to hide the Deringer in her garter again.

Frankie swallowed and looked away.

"So," Tess said when she let the dress's hem fall to her ankles, "what do we do now?"

Frankie thought about it for a while. "Make Donovan an offer," she finally said. "Tell him you want to sell him your businesses."

"No." Tess vehemently shook her head. "I won't sell, least of all to him."

"You don't have to," Frankie said. "Donovan just has to believe that you will. Set a price low enough that he can't resist, but high enough that he has to gather all his money to buy you out."

"Ah." Tess smiled. "He'll have to use the money he stole to come up with the full price. And when he goes to get the money ..."

"I'll follow him to its hiding place." Frankie tilted her head. "So, what do you say? Will you work with me?"

"On one condition," Tess answered.

Frankie studied her cautiously. "And that would be?"

"Tell me your name," Tess said. "Your real name."

Frankie had to laugh. "Frances Callaghan." Grinning, she held out her hand. "But you can call me Frankie."

"You want to sell everything?" Jeff Donovan stared at her through narrowed eyes. "I offered to buy you out a hundred times before, but you always refused. Why now?"

Quick. Come up with a plausible explanation before he becomes suspicious. "I met someone," Tess said, letting a dreamy smile play around her lips. "I want to begin a new, respectable life, and I can't do that in Independence."

"You met someone? Someone who wants to marry you?" Donovan laughed. "Where did you meet him?"

Tess smiled again. "Well, actually, we met up here." She gestured, indicating the upstairs rooms of the brothel. Her mind flashed back to the night Frankie had broken into her office.

Donovan shook his head but didn't comment.

"So?" Tess asked. "Are you interested, or do you want me to look for other buyers?"

"Of course I'm interested, but it'll take me some time to come up with all that money," Donovan said.

Tess knew she had to pressure him into acting fast. She couldn't give him the time to think and make clever plans. "I need it by tomorrow."

"Tomorrow?" Donovan echoed.

"I'm leaving town the day after tomorrow. My love wants to sweep me away on a honeymoon." Tess clutched her hands to her chest.

Donovan rolled his eyes but finally nodded. "I'll see what I can come up with on such short notice."

When he left, Tess went to her window and waved down the street.

Frankie Callaghan stepped out of the general store. She was wearing a dress this time, and she seemed as comfortable in it as she had been in male apparel.

She's not like Luke, Tess thought as she watched Frankie follow Donovan down the street. *She's not like anyone I've ever met.*

Frankie and Donovan disappeared around a corner.

Now she had to sit back and wait.

Tess sighed. Sitting around and waiting had never been her strong suit. She had argued about that with Frankie for most of the way back to Independence. Tess had finally agreed to stay behind and let Frankie handle Donovan, knowing that if he noticed Tess following him, their plan would be in vain.

Still, Tess didn't like it. All her life, she had made her own decisions and had taken action on her own. She had never depended on anyone for anything. Trusting others didn't come easily for Tess, but something about Frankie Callaghan made her decide to take the risk.

She didn't doubt Frankie's honesty or her competence. She had seen first-hand that Frankie could handle herself in a fight. Still, she couldn't help worrying. What if Donovan became suspicious and shot Frankie? What if Frankie was lying somewhere, hurt and bleeding, while Donovan escaped with the money?

Tess shook her head. *Stop it. Frankie can handle this.* With another sigh, she settled down to wait.

To all the world, Jeffrey Donovan looked like a respectable businessman as he strolled down Lexington Street, tipping his hat whenever he passed a lady.

Frankie followed at a discreet distance. *Where's he going?* She eyed the stone building at the corner. Even Donovan wouldn't be brazen—or stupid—enough to stash the stolen money in the bank, would he?

He crossed the street and disappeared into a side street.

Lifting the hem of her skirt a little so it wouldn't drag through the mud, Frankie stepped from the boardwalk and peered around the corner just in time to see Donovan enter the livery stable. Was he about to get on a horse and flee? As fast as her dress allowed, Frankie rushed toward the stable.

Her eyes took a moment to adjust to the dimmer light in the stable.

Donovan was nowhere to be seen.

Then a scraping sound caught Frankie's attention. After checking to see if the Deringer she had borrowed from Tess was still in her carpetbag, Frankie crept closer.

Horses looked back at her from the first five stalls. The last stall to the right didn't hold a horse, though.

Donovan was dragging the trough away from the wall. Breathing heavily, he removed a loose board and reached into the hole behind the wall. When he turned, he held a pair of bulging saddlebags in his hands.

"Good afternoon, Mr. Donovan," Frankie said.

He jumped. His gaze darted toward her. "Oh, Mrs. Callaghan." He tried a smile. "Nice day, isn't it?"

Oh, yeah. At least for me. Frankie nodded.

Holding the saddlebags behind his back, Donovan left the stall and tried to squeeze past Frankie.

Frankie laid one hand on his arm. "Would you mind accompanying me a bit?"

"Um, well, I'd love to, but—"

"Thank you," Frankie said. "Very kind of you." Keeping a hold of his arm, she steered them outside and back toward Lexington Street.

He struggled to free his arm. "Mrs. Callaghan, I really need to—"

"Just until we made it past the saloon and those other establishments of sin," Frankie said, fluttering her lashes like a helpless damsel in distress. "It's not safe on the streets for a woman alone nowadays."

Donovan sighed. "All right."

When they made it past the saloon, he extricated his arm from Frankie's grip.

"A little farther, please." Frankie indicated the building across the street.

Donovan's eyes narrowed as he glanced toward the sheriff's office. "What business do you have with the sheriff?"

"Oh, I don't. But you do."

He stared at her.

Frankie calmly returned his stare.

His gaze darted to the left one second before he tried to run.

"Don't move!" Frankie grabbed his arm again.

Donovan swung up the saddlebags and hit her in the face with them.

Pain flared through Frankie's lip. Warm blood dribbled down her chin. With a suppressed shout, she pulled him toward her and used the momentum to knee him between the legs.

He dropped the saddlebags and clutched himself, groaning.

Two men ran toward them. "Ma'am, did he hurt you?" one shouted, while the other grabbed Donovan by the lapels.

"He tried to steal my money." Frankie picked up the saddlebags.

One of the men shook Donovan.

"Careful," Frankie said. "Don't break his hand. He needs to sign some papers before we deliver him to the sheriff."

Independence, Missouri
September 18th, 1856

"Stop! Come back here, Mister!" Molly's sharp voice came from the hallway. "You can't just come up here and—Aren't you listening? Miss Tess doesn't receive visitors in the middle of the day."

Tess got up and opened the office door to find out what the commotion was all about.

Frankie Callaghan, back in male disguise, strode toward her, ignoring Molly, who was trying to hold her back.

"It's all right, Molly," Tess said and opened her door wider. "He's a friend of mine."

Molly stopped chasing after Frankie. "Ah." She wiggled her eyebrows.

Tess ignored her. She was too impatient to learn what had happened. As soon as she closed the door behind them, she asked, "How did it go?"

Frankie set down a pair of saddlebags on Tess's desk and opened them to reveal the money. She grinned widely despite a cut at the corner of her mouth.

Without thinking, Tess reached out. She stopped herself before her fingers could touch Frankie's lip. Except for her time with Luke, touching someone had been strictly business, an emotionless thing, for a lot of years. Where was this sudden urge to touch Frankie, even in this small way, coming from? She cleared her voice. "What happened?"

"Donovan tried to get away when he realized he was caught," Frankie said.

Tess took a deep breath. "Did he?"

"No." Frankie smiled. "He's enjoying the sheriff's

hospitality as we speak. I made him sign over the ownership of all your businesses to you before I delivered him to the sheriff."

Tess rubbed her neck. "Seems I have to find myself a new business partner."

"Why? You seem capable enough of managing on your own," Frankie said. Her brown eyes held nothing but honesty and respect.

"If word gets out that a whore owns half of Independence's best establishments, business will suffer," Tess said. "The sheriff would check on every single delivery for my businesses, taking great pleasure in delaying them." She shook her head. "Having a male partner with an honorable name makes things so much easier."

"Only if you can trust him," Frankie said.

Tess sighed. "Yeah."

Frankie was silent for a few moments. "Do you think Frank Callaghan would be trustworthy?" She gestured at her shirt-and-pants-clad body.

Tess stared at her. "You mean ... you want to be my business partner?"

"Why not?" Frankie shrugged. "I think I proved that I'm not after your money. You can be sure that I would never disrespect you just because you're a woman, and you wouldn't even have to share your money or your bed with me to ensure my loyalty."

So she knows exactly what my business relationship with Donovan entailed. Tess eyed Frankie warily. "Sounds like a good deal for me, but what's in it for you?"

"Being a Pinkerton detective can be a dangerous and strange job." Frankie held Tess's gaze. "It would be good to have a place where I could just be myself and have a friend who knew all my secrets."

Tess swallowed. To have that kind of trust put in her was scary. "Why me?"

"Because we have a lot in common," Frankie said.

Tess arched an eyebrow. "I'm a brothel madam, and you're a Pinkerton detective. How much in common could we possibly have?"

"We both play roles and pretend to be someone else for a living," Frankie said.

Tess had to look away. The understanding in Frankie's brown eyes was overwhelming. When she glanced back up, Frankie was still gazing at her. "All right," Tess said. "I'll draft a contract that says Mr. Frank Callaghan is the new owner of all the businesses for the price of ..." She winked at Frankie. "How much are you willing to pay?"

Frankie grinned and turned her pockets inside out. Only her Pinkerton badge fell out.

Tess picked it up and held the piece of metal, warm from Frankie's body heat, in her hand for a moment before handing it back. "Well, I wanted to give you a reward for bringing back my money anyway." She reached into the saddlebags for a bundle of money.

Frankie's fingers around hers stopped her. "No," Frankie said. "No reward necessary. I get paid to do my job."

"But—"

"No," Frankie said. "We Pinkerton detectives are not allowed to accept tips or rewards for our services. It's company policy, and it keeps us honest."

Tess turned her hand around and stroked the fingers that were still wrapped around her own. "No rewards, huh?"

Frankie shook her head, not taking her eyes off Tess's.

"No rewards."

Still keeping eye contact, Tess stepped closer until her body was almost touching Frankie's. "So I shouldn't do this?" She lifted her face.

"Well," Frankie murmured, her breath hot on Tess's lips, "I guess it would be all right if you kissed your new business partner and not the Pinkerton detective."

Tess slid her fingers up Frankie's neck, buried them in Frankie's short hair, and pulled her unresisting business partner down. "Deal," she whispered before her lips were otherwise occupied.

###

THE CHRISTMAS OAK

Author's note

Christmas wasn't declared a federal holiday until 1870, and in the 1850s, Christmas trees weren't very common in the West yet.

Hamilton Horse Ranch
Baker Prairie, Oregon
December 24th, 1857

"Christmas tree?" Luke repeated. She'd never heard of such a thing.

Nora looked up from the pie dough she was kneading on the kitchen table. "Yes. I saw a picture in a magazine. Apparently, having a Christmas tree is all the rage back east. It's usually a fir or a pine. About this tall." When she lifted her hand to indicate the tree's size, flour rained down on her, dusting her red hair. Now she looked as if she were covered in snow.

Smiling, Luke walked over and smoothed her hands over the soft strands. She kissed flour off Nora's nose. "You really want me to ride out in this weather to drag home a tree?"

"I thought it might make a nice family tradition." Nora slid her arms around Luke and kissed her, then moved back a few inches. She looked up at Luke with an earnest expression. "But if you think the weather's too bad ..."

Luke wouldn't be able to say no even if a blizzard had been wreaking havoc outside. "The weather is no problem," she said. "I'll check on Amy's present while I'm searching for that Christmas tree."

"Mama, Papa, look!" Nattie's voice from the parlor interrupted them in the middle of another kiss.

"I'll go," Luke said. She stole a piece of dough and walked into the parlor.

Six-year-old Nattie pressed her nose against the parlor windowpane and peered outside. "It's still raining." She turned and scrunched her forehead. "Will Santa Claus come if there's no snow? His sleigh needs snow."

Amy joined her sister at the window. "Why doesn't he just use horses instead of reindeer?"

Luke suppressed a laugh. Like any rancher's daughter, Amy thought most problems could be solved by a good horse. "Don't worry, you two. Santa doesn't need snow. His reindeer can fly."

"Ooh!" Nattie stared at her with wide-eyed awe.

Amy glanced back and forth between Luke and the rain outside, one eyebrow forming a skeptical arch. "Hannah says there ain't no Santa Claus."

Nattie stomped her foot. "Yes, there is! Take that back."

Quickly, Luke stepped between them. "No arguing on Christmas Eve, girls. Why don't you wait until tomorrow morning? If there are gifts in your stockings, then I guess we'll know Santa really exists." Luke wanted them to believe in Santa Claus for a little while longer, maybe because she had never gotten to celebrate Christmas as a child. Christmas was a family celebration, and living with

94

her drunken mother in a brothel, Luke hadn't been part of a real family. Now she enjoyed the wonders of Christmas through her daughters' eyes.

She put on her coat and gloves and took her hat from the peg next to the door.

"Where are you going?" Amy left her place next to the window.

"Looking for a Christmas tree."

"Ooh!" Amy's eyes shone. "The picture in Mama's book looks so pretty. Can I come and help pick one?"

Nattie hurried over. "Me too?"

Luke stood helplessly staring down at them. Normally, she loved taking the girls with her, but if she said yes now, she'd spoil the surprise of Amy's Christmas present. "Not this time. It's raining too hard."

The two disappointed little faces made her flinch.

"Who wants to lick the spoon?" Nora called from the kitchen.

"Me!" Nattie shouted.

"No, me!"

As their daughters rushed from the parlor, Luke blew out a breath. *Good timing, love.* She put on her hat and stepped out into the rain to hunt for the perfect Christmas tree.

* * *

Luke carefully directed Measles down a muddy slope. The mare was getting older, but she was still sure-footed. "Where is that grandson of yours hiding, old girl?"

Measles flicked her ears back but didn't answer.

Rain dripped off her hat's brim. Shivering, Luke pulled up her coat collar.

Finally, beneath a stand of trees, she made out a band of horses. Three mares stood with their heads together, seeking shelter from the wind and rain. A few yearlings chased each other through the wet grass. Two of them rolled around in the mud. When they saw Luke, they scrambled to their feet and shook themselves. Mud spattered in all directions.

Luke's gaze skipped from horse to horse, searching for a particular one—the red-dusted colt Nattie had named Cinnamon. "There he is."

At Luke and Measles's approach, Cinnamon lifted his head and looked up from his mouthful of grass. His gaze veered to his mother, the lead mare, but he didn't run.

Good. A calm horse is just what I need for Amy.

When his mother, a red mare named Cayenne, had been born, Luke had promised Amy that the mare's first foal would be hers. Cayenne's colt had been born late in the year. When the other foals were weaned from their mothers, he hadn't been old enough, but now it was time. She'd check him out now to make sure he looked his best, and then tomorrow she would ride out with Amy and bring him home.

Just as Luke swung her leg over the cantle, she caught movement out of the corner of her eye. One foot still in the stirrup, she paused and scanned the area.

Nothing moved. Only the Molalla River gurgled on its way north.

Had she imagined the movement?

Luke had long since learned to trust her instincts. She grabbed her rifle and dropped down. Over Measles's back, she again slid her gaze over the valley. Her skin prickled with the feeling of being watched.

She focused on the line shack near the river. She had

built it three years ago, when she hired her first ranch hand. But right now, the ranch's riders were repairing the fence on their south pasture, so the line shack was supposed to be empty.

Nothing moved in the small corral, but smoke curled up from the cabin's chimney.

Someone's in there. She checked her rifle before she made her way over to the line shack, using the cover of the trees. Her rifle raised, ready to fire, she nudged the door with one boot.

The door creaked open.

Luke held her breath and peeked inside.

The cabin's one room lay empty.

She released the air from her lungs and lowered her rifle but kept it cradled in the bend of her arm as she entered the cabin.

Wood smoke engulfed her. A quick touch showed that the hearth was still warm. Water dripped from the logs in the fireplace.

Luke frowned. Had someone quickly doused the fire when he'd seen her coming, not realizing that dousing the fire would create even more smoke?

A blanket had obviously been used and now hung over the edge of the cot as if someone had hurriedly tossed it there.

Had a traveler slept in the line shack and left in a hurry to make it home in time for Christmas? She had nothing against strangers using the cabin for a night or two. They were even welcome to some of the food as long as they left enough money to replace it.

She stepped over to the rough-hewn shelf and checked the provisions.

Some of the smoked bacon was gone, and the bag of

after him.

Luke struggled to keep her footing. Mud splashed her calves and slid inside her boots, and she lost her hat as she leaped over a creek. Cold rain lashed her face.

Damn, he's fast. She gritted her teeth and tried to speed up. It wouldn't do for Lucas Hamilton, successful rancher, to be outrun by a mere boy.

The boy reached the top of the hill. His foot slipped out from under him, and he fell. He slid down the hill on the seat of his pants. When he skidded to a stop at the bottom of the hill, he jumped to his feet.

Luke leaped and tackled the boy just as he regained his footing.

They both went down and rolled around in a tangle of limbs and mud.

Instead of lying still, the boy fought like a cougar.

A fist hit Luke's ear.

"Ouch. Stop fighting me." She managed to capture his wrists in both hands, but she needed her full weight and all her strength to keep him from bucking her off. Once again, Luke was reminded that in a physical fight, she was no match for a grown man. She had enough trouble keeping this boy from bashing her head in. "Goddammit, lie still. I don't want to hurt you. I'm not even handing you over to the sheriff. I just want to—"

He thrust his knee between her legs.

The padding in her pants softened the blow, but pain still shot through her. Groaning, she lost her grip on the boy.

He slithered out from beneath her and struggled to his feet.

Air returned to Luke's lungs just in time for her to grab his leg.

The boy went down again.

Panting, Luke rolled around and held him down, this time making sure to immobilize his legs by sitting on them. *Whoever said a kick between the legs is only painful for men is a goddamn liar.*

Despite her firm grip, the boy never stopped struggling. His blue eyes were frozen with fear, and his wild gaze seemed to stare right through her, maybe seeing something in his past.

"Stop! Stop it, boy. I won't hurt you. I'll let you up if you don't try to run away again."

The boy threw his weight against Luke once more, then sank into the mud and lay still. His chest heaved as he sucked in a breath. "All right."

"Promise not to run?"

His mud-crusted lashes blinked up at her as if he was surprised that anyone would trust his word. Finally, he nodded.

Luke rolled off him.

Gasping, they sat side by side in the mud.

"Why did you run?"

The boy shrugged.

He doesn't trust me. Probably doesn't trust anyone. "Come on. Let's go get cleaned up and get some food in you." She got to her feet and reached down to help him up.

The boy hesitated, but then he took her hand and let himself be pulled to his feet.

* * *

Luke stepped onto the porch and dragged off her mud-covered boots. She gave a nod to the boy, who stood

101

silently watching her. "Take off your boots outside," she said, "or my wife will have both our hides."

Visibly paling, the boy took off his boots and placed them next to Luke's on the veranda.

When Luke opened the door, Amy hurried over. Her gaze traveled over Luke's empty hands. "No Christmas tree?" The welcoming smile slid off her face and was replaced by a frown.

Oh. Luke had forgotten all about the tree.

Then Amy saw the stranger. Fearlessly, she stepped forward and looked up at the taller boy. "Hello. I'm Amy. Who are you?"

The boy looked at Luke as if asking for help, and she gave him a nod of encouragement.

"I'm Phin." He shook the hand Amy held out to him and then stepped back.

Nora stepped out of the bedroom, one arm around Nattie, who was shyly clutching her mother's skirt. She took in the scene in her parlor. "It looks like you two need a change of clothes."

Luke smiled. How typically Nora. She didn't ask who the boy was and what had happened for them to be covered in mud; she just saw a boy in need and offered help, trusting that she'd get the whole story later.

And Luke knew she would tell her everything, not even leaving out the embarrassing mud wrestling and the kick between the legs.

* * *

Luke leaned back in her chair at the head of the table and watched Nora heap ham and potatoes onto Phin's plate.

The boy shoveled down food as if he hadn't eaten in weeks, barely chewing or looking at what he was eating. His gaze darted back and forth between the two ranch hands, who were regaling Amy with stories about wild horses, and Nattie, who chatted on and on about the gifts she might find in her stocking tomorrow.

"Phin." Nora touched his arm to get his attention.

Phin paused with the fork half way to his mouth and stared at the hand on his arm. He didn't lean into the gentle touch, but he didn't move away from it either.

He doesn't trust men, but he's got no problem with women, Luke thought. How ironic that Phin had flinched away from her.

"Where are you from?" Nora asked.

The noise level at the table instantly went down, and silence spread as everyone waited for the answer.

Phin slowed his chewing and swallowed heavily. "Up north," he said, pointing vaguely with his fork.

"Canada?" Nora asked.

Phin moved his head in a half-circle that could mean yes or no.

"And no one is traveling with you? You're all alone?"

This time Phin nodded. "I'm almost fifteen. I can take care of myself."

Luke had been on her own at an even younger age, but she still remembered the many nights she went to sleep with an empty stomach and the many nights she'd forced herself to stay awake, listening into the early hours for bandits out to steal her belongings. She'd finally joined the dragoons to end her loneliness and aimless drifting. Of course, with the Mexican War still going on, becoming a soldier had been a jump out of the frying pan right into the fire.

"And you've got no family left?" Nora asked. "No one who'd worry about you when you don't come home?"

"No one," Phin said between two forkfuls of ham.

Nora took in the fading bruises on his face and exchanged a glance with Luke. Her green eyes shone with unshed tears.

Luke reached out and squeezed her hand beneath the table. *Don't take this on yourself, darling. You can't suffer with every homeless child who comes along, or it'll break your heart.*

"Do you want a roast apple?" Nora asked.

The tense set of Phin's shoulders loosened when the questions about him stopped. He nodded eagerly.

Nora took an apple from its place over the fire, sprinkled cinnamon over it, and set it down in front of Phin.

"Don't burn your tongue," Nattie said, sounding so much like Nora that everyone laughed.

Little fists pounding against the bedroom door jerked Luke awake.

"Mama! Papa," Nattie and Amy shouted, but, as they had been taught, the girls didn't open the door.

Nora slipped out of bed. She leaned down to kiss Luke's cheek. "Go get dressed. I'll distract them until you're ready to join us."

Ten minutes later, when Luke stepped out of the bedroom, breasts bound beneath her shirt and vest, Amy and Nattie jumped up and down in the parlor.

"Papa." Nattie grabbed her hand and dragged her over to the window. "Look. It snowed."

It wasn't the mountains of snow Luke had grown up with back east, but a bit of snow had fallen overnight. Now three inches of snow covered the corral, the tree branches, and the hills around the ranch. "So Santa shouldn't have had any problems delivering presents last night," Luke said. "Maybe you should go check your stockings."

"Wait." Nora laid one hand on each of the girls' shoulders, then glanced at Luke. "Can you go and get Phin first? From the look of things, I bet he never got to celebrate Christmas before."

Luke went over to the bunkhouse, where Phin had spent the night.

When she opened the door, Toby was putting a new log into the cast-iron stove. Hank sat on his bunk, but the two other beds were empty.

"Where's the boy?" Luke asked.

"Gone," Hank said. "He'd already left when I woke

up."

Luke trudged back through the snow to the main house, trying to find the right words to explain it to her family. The girls would be disappointed. They had wanted to show off their presents to the newcomer, and Nora had wanted to spoil him with good food and motherly warmth on Christmas.

A strange noise from the ranch yard made her turn around before she reached the veranda.

There, in the middle of the ranch yard, stood Phin. Sweat shone on his brow, and one sleeve of his threadbare coat was ripped. Both of his hands were wrapped around the slender trunk of a young white oak.

Luke squinted over at him. "What are you doing?"

Slowly, Phin crossed the ranch yard and propped the tree up against the veranda railing. Brown leaves bobbed up and down on the ash-gray branches. "Thought since you forgot the Christmas tree because of me, I'd get one." He nodded down at the tree, cautious pride glowing in his eyes.

Oh, Lord. Luke bit back a laugh. *Guess we should have told him that Christmas trees are usually pines or firs.* She reached out to give him a pat on the shoulder, but when he flinched back, she settled for a nod of appreciation. "Let's get your tree inside. You're just in time for presents."

* * *

A tug on her sleeve made Luke look away from Phin and Nora, who were trying to find the best place for their Christmas oak.

"Papa." Nattie pointed to the tree. "That's not how the Christmas trees look in the pictures."

"Ssssh." Luke pressed a finger to her lips. "Phin didn't know that. You don't want to hurt his feelings by telling him he brought us the wrong tree, do you?"

Black braids flew when Nattie shook her head. "It'll be a secret," she whispered. "Maybe next year, Amy and I can help him pick the right tree."

Next year. Luke paused but didn't want to lie. Since she couldn't tell their daughters the ultimate truth about herself, she'd sworn to at least be truthful about everything else. "Sweetie, Phin won't be here next year."

"Why not?"

"Nattie," Nora called before Luke could answer. "Come help decorate the tree."

When Nattie hurried off, Luke blew out a breath. *Saved again.*

Nora walked over and joined her, perching on the edge of Luke's armchair.

Luke slung one arm around Nora's hip, holding her safely, and leaned her head against Nora's.

Together, they watched the girls hang apples and straw stars onto the oak branches. Phin picked up Nattie so that she could place a little doll on top of the tree. When he put Nattie back down, she threw her arms around his waist and hugged him.

He stiffened and stared down at her as if her arms were poisonous snakes slithering up his body, but then he slowly reached out and put his hand on her shoulder.

Nora chuckled. "He reminds me of you."

"Me?"

"That's exactly how you looked when Amy hugged you for the first time." Nora's grin disappeared, and she looked into Luke's eyes. "He's starved for love."

Luke closed her eyes. She knew what was coming.

"Can't we take him in and give him a home?"

"Nora." Luke opened her eyes. "I don't know if that's a good idea."

"Why not? Surely letting him stay with us would be better than letting him fend for himself."

The armchair creaked as Luke turned to face Nora. "It would be a big risk for me. One more person around who could find out who and what I really am."

"You took the same risk when you hired Toby and Hank," Nora said. She rubbed Luke's shoulder, tenderly massaging her tense muscles. "What's this really about?"

Luke squeezed the bridge of her nose while she tried to give voice to her feelings. "Toby and Hank are adults. Phin is still a boy."

"And?"

"If we take him in, he might look to me as a father figure. A role model. I'm not sure I'm ready for that."

Nora slid closer, now almost sitting on Luke's lap. She frowned down at Luke. "But you're a wonderful father for Amy and Nattie. You don't still doubt that, do you?"

"No. But Amy and Nattie are girls. They'll model themselves after you."

"Oh, yeah?" Nora laughed. "When I was ten, I didn't wish for a horse for Christmas. Amy takes after you just as much as she takes after me."

A smile trembled on Luke's lips. The thought was as scary as it was elating. "Yes, but still, the girls will learn what it means to be a woman from you." She lowered her voice to an almost inaudible whisper. "How can I teach Phin how to be a man when I'm ..." Gesturing down her body, she fell silent.

"How about teaching him how to be a decent human being first?"

"Yes, but—"

"Tell me one thing a man could teach him that you can't," Nora said, her voice low, but firm.

Luke's thoughts skipped from idea to idea like a flat stone over the surface of a lake. Riding. Fighting. Gentling a horse. Building a cabin. Shaving. Protecting the weak. Treating women with respect.

She'd done all of that many times.

Surprised, she looked into Nora's eyes. Could she really do this?

"A boy could have a worse role model," Nora said. "In fact, I suspect that his father beat him."

Luke's stomach clenched at the thought.

"Mama, Papa, look," Amy shouted from across the parlor. "The tree is ready. Can we open our presents now?"

There, next to Nora's rolltop desk, stood the merriest oak Luke had ever seen. Its branches hung low with nuts, apples, cookies, straw stars, and colorful ribbons.

"Sometimes," Nora whispered, "an oak makes the best Christmas tree. And sometimes, a woman makes the best father figure." She kissed Luke's temple and walked across the room to help Nattie take her stocking down from the mantle.

Stunned, Luke stayed behind.

Phin wandered over to her, hands stuffed in his pockets. "I better go now. Thanks for the food."

A squeal from Amy distracted Luke. She looked across the room and saw Amy hold a new wooden horse in her hands. Amy ran her hands over its red-dusted coat.

Luke grinned. *Just wait until you find out we're giving you a real-life horse for Christmas too.*

When Luke turned her head back around, the boy was

gone.

She jumped up from the armchair, crossed the room in three quick strides, and threw the door open. "Phin!"

He turned on the top step of the veranda.

Luke cleared her throat. "Why don't you stay?"

"Christmas is for families," Phin said.

"That's why we want you to stay."

Now Phin turned fully and stared at her. "I told you I can take care of myself. I don't need your pity."

Tread carefully. Don't hurt his pride. "I'm not offering pity. I'm offering ..." She hesitated, and then her gaze fell on the bunkhouse. "I'm offering a job."

"A job?"

"You any good with horses?"

Phin shrugged.

Luke decided to take it as a yes. "Good. Then you're hired. If you want the job."

The wooden step creaked as Phin shifted his weight. He met Luke's gaze, silently probing. Then he nodded. "I want it."

"Then come on." Luke held open the door, and she could already feel Nora's proud gaze rest on her. "I think there's a stocking in the parlor with your name on it."

Phin stepped past her, this time not flinching away from her light touch to his shoulder.

For a moment, Luke stayed behind, silently taking in her family gathered around the Christmas oak. Then she grinned and went inside to join them.

###

SWEPT AWAY

Hamilton Horse Ranch
Baker Prairie, Oregon
December 3rd, 1861

The front door banged open.

Amy nearly dropped the plates she was carrying to the table when Papa rushed inside.

For once, he didn't bother to take off his hat. Water dripped onto the wooden floor.

"Papa!" Amy abandoned the plates. "What happened?"

Mama hurried over from the stove and tried to help Papa out of his wet coat.

"No." Papa shook his head. "I'll need to go out again in a minute. I just came in to tell you that I won't be home for supper. The river is still rising, and this damn rain isn't gonna stop anytime soon. I need to drive the yearlings to the south pasture, away from the river, or they might drown."

Amy ran to get her coat and hat. "I'll help you."

Papa took the hat and coat from her and hung them back on the peg next to the door. "No. I'll take Phin with me. You stay here."

"But—"

"Your mother could use your help here," Papa said.

Amy stomped her foot. "Setting the table for supper?"

She snorted. Rescuing the yearlings was much more important than household tasks. "Just because I'm a girl, I have to stay here and set the stupid table while Phin—"

Papa stepped closer and lowered his head to stare directly into her eyes. "This has nothing to do with you being a girl. Phin's an adult. You're fourteen. That's why he's coming with me, and you're staying here."

Amy's shoulders slumped.

After patting Amy's arm, Papa kissed Mama, and then he was gone.

Great. Amy sank into Papa's favorite armchair and leaned her head on her hands. Now the waiting began.

* * *

Hoofbeats drowned out the drumming of rain on the roof.

Amy's head jerked up. *Is Papa back already?* She rushed to the window, one of the few in the valley that had an actual glass pane.

Clouds hung low, throwing shadows onto the ranch yard. Amy squinted to see through the rain-smeared glass. After a second, she made out the contours of a buckboard. "Mama," she called. "Someone's coming."

Her mother was already opening the door, a rifle in her hand.

Amy followed quickly before Mama could tell her to stay back.

In the ranch yard, Jacob Garfield handed his wife and daughter down from the buckboard. Bernice and Hannah lifted their skirts and waded through ankle-deep puddles.

"Hannah!" Amy's heart began to race. She ran to open the door.

The Garfields rushed into the parlor.

"I'm sorry to barge in on you like this," Bernice said, "but—"

Mama stopped her with a wave of her hand. "You know we don't mind."

Amy surely didn't. She hadn't seen Hannah in weeks. Every time she had gone to town, Hannah had to help in her parents' store or had been busy with other things. It seemed like forever since they had last gone riding together.

Mama turned to Amy. "Amy, take Hannah up to your room and give her one of your dresses to change into. The poor girl is soaked to the bones."

She was. Her bodice clung to her ample chest. From beneath her sunbonnet, her dark hair hung down in sodden strands.

"That would be wonderful," Hannah said. She gave Amy a weak smile. "Days like this I reckon wearing pants like you do wouldn't be so bad after all."

Amy reached for Hannah's hand to lead her to her room. Hannah's hand was cold, and Amy rubbed it between hers to warm it on the way upstairs. While they climbed the stairs, she strained to hear the conversation in the parlor, but she couldn't make out more than a few words.

Nattie peeked out of her room as they passed, an open book in her hands. "What's going on?"

"I don't know yet," Amy said.

Nattie followed them to Amy's room and sat on the bed.

Ignoring her little sister, Amy poured water from a pitcher into the bowl on the washstand and placed a towel and a piece of soap next to it. "Here. I hope you like the soap." Mama's friend Tess had sent the perfumed soap from the East, and Amy had saved it for a special occasion.

"Thank you. It smells nice." Hannah draped her soaked shawl over a trunk at the foot of Amy's bed and started to unbutton her bodice.

Amy quickly turned away and busied herself with finding a dress Hannah could wear. Her cheeks burned, and she cursed herself. Hannah was her best friend, so why was she suddenly blushing around her? "What are you doing out in this weather?" she asked when she was sure her voice would sound normal.

"We wanted to visit the Buchanans," Hannah said. Fabric rustled. A light green skirt was placed next to the shawl on the trunk, then three petticoats followed.

Still not looking at Hannah, Amy eyed the skirt and petticoats. Was Hannah wearing her Sunday best in the middle of the week? "In this rain?"

"It's been raining for the past two weeks. Mama didn't want to put off the visit any longer."

"Then what brings you here?" The Buchanans' farm didn't border directly at the Hamilton outfit.

Hannah put her damp stockings onto the trunk. "The roads are much worse than we thought. The buckboard almost got stuck twice in the mud." She stepped closer to Amy. "Can you help me with the corset?"

Heat rushed through Amy. She nodded, not trusting her voice, and slowly turned. So Hannah was really wearing her Sunday finery, including a corset. Willing her fingers not to tremble, Amy reached out to loosen the laces in the back of the corset. Her gaze followed the curve of Hannah's shoulder blades. How pale and smooth Hannah's skin was.

"Amy?"

"Uh, yes?" Amy wrenched her gaze away and quickly loosened the rest of the laces. "So you want to stay until the rain lets up?"

"Oh, that would be nice," Nattie said from the bed. "You could tell us all the news from town. Did your father get any new books in?"

"I don't know," Hannah said and turned to face them, clutching the corset to her breasts. "I was busy with other things."

Was that a blush spreading over Hannah's cheeks and extending down to her upper chest? Amy wasn't sure. She didn't dare look too closely for fear Hannah might think she was ogling her.

"We probably won't stay the night. Papa just wanted to ask your father for help." Hannah took the skirt and blouse Amy held out to her and turned away. "Two of the bridges have been swept away, and Papa is afraid that the Buchanans might not be doing so good."

Amy looked out the window. The rain still hadn't let up. Their pastures had turned into mud. The first cut of hay might be ruined for next year, but at least the Hamilton Ranch wasn't in any immediate danger. Papa had built their main house and the outbuildings in a safe spot, on a hill, not too close to the river.

Some of their neighbors hadn't had the same foresight. The Buchanans had built their home on the banks of the Willamette River. While that provided them with easy access to a source of water, their location also put them at risk whenever the river was rising.

"The Buchanans might be in trouble. Your father is right about that." Amy chewed on her lip. She wished Papa were home to tell her what to do. "We've got to check on them."

"Amy," Mama called from the parlor. "You make supper for Nattie and Hannah while I go with Bernice and Jacob to check on the Buchanans."

Amy gritted her teeth. Why did her parents always try to make her stay home? "Nattie can make supper," she called back. She raced downstairs to send Mama her most pleading gaze. "I'll come with you. I know every inch of land between here and the Buchanans' farm."

Mama hesitated. She looked at Jacob, who shrugged.

Hannah stepped next to Amy. "I'm coming with you too."

"Lord." Jacob groaned. "What happened to the good old days when daughters were content to stay home and do whatever their parents told them to do?"

Mama laughed. "It never worked like that in our family, Jacob." She looked at Amy, then gazed out the window. "All right. We'll all go. If the Buchanans are really in trouble, likely they could use every helping hand."

* * *

The Garfields piled onto the buckboard, while Mama, Nattie, and Amy saddled horses for themselves.

Normally, Amy preferred for Hannah to climb into the saddle behind her. Whenever Hannah slid her hands around her and held on to Amy's waist, Amy felt like a knight in one of Nattie's books. But now with the soaked ground, Cinnamon couldn't carry the double weight.

Amy squinted in the rain to make out mud holes.

Cinnamon snorted.

Amy patted his wet neck. "I don't like this weather either, Cin."

The closer they came to the Buchanans' land and the

river, the worse it got. The fields ahead were flooded and the wheat, which should have been harvested soon, ruined. In some places, the fences were inundated to above the bottom rail.

Cinnamon waded up a hill. At the crest, Amy reined in the gelding and stared ahead.

In the distance, the Willamette River and its tributaries formed one big, mile-wide lake.

"Oh, Lord," Hannah said. "I hope Joshua's all right. He can't swim."

Amy pressed her lips together. She couldn't swim either, and it hurt that Hannah was only thinking of him, not of her. *Well, you're not living right next to the river.*

Jacob urged the horse in front of the buckboard forward.

Amy stayed to the side of the buckboard so the mud flung up by the wagon wheels wouldn't hit Cinnamon.

A dead cow drifted in the knee-deep water to their right.

Amy sent a glance skyward. *Lord, please let Papa and the yearlings be all right.*

Keeping to the highest points that weren't as flooded, they made their way upstream toward the Buchanans' farm.

Debris rushed down the roaring river. Two sheep were swept northward; then a pile of wood whirled by.

Lights danced on the river and quickly came closer.

Amy stared. *Is that ...?* She clutched the reins more tightly. "It's the Buchanans' house!"

The raging flood had picked up the whole house. With the lights still burning, it floated down the river. As the house passed them, Amy saw a shadow move inside. "Someone's still inside!" She urged Cinnamon into a faster gait, chasing after the house.

Mama and Nattie quickly caught up with her. The buckboard rumbled through the mud behind them. Bernice repeated the Lord's Prayer over and over.

The water rose up Cinnamon's legs, so Amy steered him farther away from the river but kept an eye on the floating house.

The house crashed against the riverbank and shook as if it was about to burst.

Amy held her breath.

Bernice's prayer grew louder, almost drowning out the roaring waters.

Rain poured off Amy's hat as she tilted her head and peered through the torrents. The house wasn't dragged downstream any farther. "It's lodged among the hazelnut bushes!"

They left behind horses and wagon and dashed through the mud toward the house.

The porch was pointing away from them, so there was no easy way inside.

"I'll climb inside," Jacob shouted. "You women stay here." He forced up the window and leaned on the sill to climb inside.

The branches of the hazelnut bush creaked.

"No," Amy shouted. "You're too heavy. If you climb inside, the house will be swept away. Let me go."

Jacob paused and stared at her. "But you're just a girl."

Papa would have never said that, but he wasn't here now, so Amy had to grit her teeth and deal with Jacob. "Yes, I'm a girl," she said, forcing herself not to let her annoyance show. "That's why I'm lighter than you. Uncle Jacob, please. Let me do this."

Jacob looked back and forth between the house and

Amy.

"Come here, Amy," Mama shouted over the roar of the water.

"No, Mama, I—"

"Come here!"

Amy turned.

Mama reached around her, slung a lariat around Amy's middle, and tied it off with a knot Papa had shown them. She kissed Amy's forehead. "Now go. And be careful."

Jacob still blocked the window. "Are you sure you want her to—?"

"Yes." Mama pushed at his shoulder.

Finally, Jacob took hold of the lariat's end and moved away.

Amy's stomach knotted. *Don't think. Just move.* After one glance back at the women at the river's bank, Amy crawled through the window. She set her feet onto the floor of the Buchanans' bedroom, careful not to cause any vibrations that might dislodge the house from its precarious hold. Wood creaked, but the bushes still held on to the house.

Amy tiptoed forward. Water swirled around her ankles. She looked around.

The wooden trunk that normally sat at the foot of the bed had been swept halfway toward the door. Someone had piled the Buchanans' most valuable possessions onto the bed to save them from the rising water. A leather-bound Bible balanced on top of Sunday dresses, a rifle, and a hand-carved cradle. A doll was perched on the pile as if watching everything.

Amy opened the bedroom door and looked around the parlor.

It was empty too.

Had she been mistaken and only imagined someone moving inside the house? *Mama will have my hide if I'm risking my life for nothing.*

But then a low whimper came from the parlor.

"Hello?" Amy called.

No answer came.

Slowly, step by step, Amy crossed the parlor, letting the whimpers guide her.

The noises were clearly coming from the fireplace, which was as wet as the rest of the parlor.

Was an animal, swept into the house by the flood, stuck there?

Amy crouched down to look into the fireplace.

Wide blue eyes stared back at her.

"Lucinda!" Amy let her gaze sweep over the Buchanans' youngest daughter, making sure she wasn't hurt. "What are you doing here? Where are your parents?"

Instead of answering, Lucinda launched herself at Amy.

Amy was toppled over and landed on the floor, the six-year-old on top of her. Water soaked her through her pants and shirt.

The house creaked and shook.

Amy's heart lurched. "Lucy," she whispered. "Stay very, very still."

The floor tilted beneath them. They tumbled toward the front door, which stood open, revealing the roaring river beyond.

Amy protectively clutched the girl against her body. She tried to stop their slide, digging in her heels. It was to no avail. They rushed toward the door and the river.

No, no, no! Amy grabbed hold of the table, but it was hurled toward the river too.

A jerk on the rope around Amy's middle stopped their fall.

Air whooshed out of Amy's lungs. She lay still, gasping, then the groaning of the house made her fly into action. With trembling fingers, she loosened the knot, holding on to the rope with one hand. She tied it around Lucinda's thin waist and frantically pulled on the rope, hoping Jacob and Mama on the other end would understand that she wanted them to pull.

Branches broke outside.

A pull on the rope jerked them toward the bedroom, but it wasn't fast enough.

The house slid slowly back into the river. Amy's weight on top of Lucinda's was slowing them down. As they were dragged through the bedroom door, she let go of the rope.

Lucinda was wrenched away, toward the window. She screamed at the top of her lungs.

With a bursting sound, the house was pulled back into the floods, away from the bank.

* * *

Everything seemed to happen at the same time. Lucinda was yanked through the window. Amy crashed to the floor and held on to the doorjamb. The house around her spun and bucked like a bronco.

Hold on!

Debris hit the house, making it shake. With an almost painful squeal, one of the walls was wrenched away. Gasping, fighting down panic, Amy knelt on the now raft-like structure and stared at the roaring torrent surrounding her. The banks rushed by. All she could see was the torrent of gushing, brownish water.

Screams and shouts, almost drowned out by the roaring water, came from outside.

Mama!

A lump formed in Amy's throat, choking her. Her hands shook so much that she almost lost her grip on the doorjamb. She was trapped. No way out. Her only chance was to hope the house would lodge in a tree or a bush along the banks again.

Ahead of her, she made out a bend in the river. The house was swept toward the riverbank. If she got close enough, maybe—just maybe—she could jump ashore.

Please, please, please!

The house crashed against the bank. Amy was hurled across the room. Her head collided with the bed. She cried out and covered her head with her arms. The cradle toppled over, almost hitting her too. Lucinda's doll landed next to her.

Groaning, Amy looked up.

Part of the outer wall had been torn away. The remnants of the house bobbed up and down just a few yards from the riverbank.

Following an impulse, Amy shoved the doll behind her waistband and staggered toward the opening in the wall. Right before the edge, she stopped. The bank was too far away to reach it by jumping. Could she make it the five yards to the bank if she paddled like crazy?

Her legs trembled as she tightened her muscles and prepared to jump.

"Amy, no!"

Amy's head jerked up. Hot tears dribbled down her face as she made out Papa, standing in the stirrups on top of Dancer, waving frantically. Her legs gave in, and she fell to the floor. "Papa, help me!"

"Stay calm," Papa shouted. "I'll come and get you." He jumped off his horse, slid down the muddy bank, and waded into the river.

The floods tore at his legs, nearly sweeping him away.

Cursing, he jumped back. "The current is too strong. Whatever you do, don't jump in."

The house moved faster now, away from Papa. "Papa!"

Papa raced along the bank, jumping over driftwood and other debris.

The river made another bend, forcing the house toward the opposite bank, where Papa wouldn't be able to reach it anymore.

Papa jumped into the water.

"Nooo!" Amy shouted as waves crashed over his head. She couldn't see him anymore. "Papa? Papa!" On her knees, she slid closer to the edge of the improvised raft and stared into the brownish flood.

Her father was gone.

Amy sobbed.

A touch to her knee made her look up.

Papa! He clung to the wooden floor of the house. "Slide down to me and climb onto my back."

"B-but I'm too heavy." Amy stared at the river. What if she dragged Papa down too?

Water dripped from Papa's hair. "Remember how I saved your mother from the Wakarusa River?"

Amy nodded. It was one of few things she could remember of her early childhood. Mama had almost drowned, trying to prevent Amy's doll from falling into the river. Amy gripped the doll sticking out from her pants.

"I can do this," Papa said as if to reassure them both.

Hesitatingly, Amy slid down and climbed onto his back. She wrapped her arms around his shoulders and held on for dear life.

"Whatever you do, don't let go," Papa said. Then he pushed them away from the remnants of the house.

Rushing water tore at them, engulfed them.

Amy's head dipped under water. She couldn't breathe. Panic rose. She struggled against the urge to let go and kick her arms and legs. Water burned in her eyes. She couldn't see and didn't even know which way was up and which was down.

Something slammed into her back. Her mouth opened as she wanted to cry out in pain. Instead, she swallowed water. Her lungs ached.

Papa's strong legs propelled them up.

Amy's head broke the surface. She spat out water and gasped for air, sucking it into her lungs.

Inch by inch, Papa brought them closer to shore.

Amy kicked out her legs to help. A wave washed over them, and she swallowed more water.

Papa coughed beneath her, but he never stopped swimming. Finally, he crawled up the riverbank.

Amy rolled off his back, panting, coughing.

They lay in the mud, just gasping for air and staring into the cloudy sky.

Then Papa sat up and looked at her. Water ran down his face. "What the heck were you doing in that house?"

"L-l-lucinda." Amy's teeth clacked against each other. She was trembling so much that she could barely speak.

Papa stared at her.

"T-the B-buchanan's daughter," Amy said. "She w-was stuck in the house. I rescued her, b-but then it was too late for me to get out."

"Christ, if I hadn't come down to the river to look for the yearlings ..." Papa's voice trembled too. "Never, ever do something like this again, do you hear me?"

Amy flung herself at her father. She burrowed her head against his shoulder, ignoring the wet, muddy shirt, and cried.

* * *

They wandered south, keeping a safe distance from the river. Amy shivered in her wet clothes. They crested yet another hill, but still no trace of Papa's horse or anyone coming to their rescue. All Amy could see was water, mud, and ruined fields. Apparently, the river had swept her northward for quite a distance.

"Where's Phin?" she asked. Maybe he would find Dancer, the gelding Papa had left behind, and come get them. She longed to climb onto the gelding's back and let him carry her home.

"I sent him to see if any of the yearlings went down to the Molalla."

He had barely finished the sentence when hoofbeats approached.

Amy stumbled and stopped.

The Garfields' buckboard rumbled toward them. Mama galloped ahead on Cinnamon, her own mare in tow. Her hair had come free from its pins and was fluttering like a red flag in the wind. She brought the gelding to a stop in front of them and slid from the saddle. Her face was blotchy as if she had been crying.

"I'm all right, Ma—"

Mama engulfed her in a tight hug, muffling the rest of what Amy wanted to say.

The Garfields and the Buchanans crowded around them, all talking at the same time, asking, explaining, laughing, and crying.

Finally, Amy's strained nerves couldn't take it anymore. She freed herself from Mama's embrace and walked over to the Buchanans.

Tom and his wife Emeline were huddled together, holding on to Lucinda, while Joshua, Tom's grown son, hovered nearby.

"I don't know how to thank you," Tom said, his voice rough as if he had been shouting for hours. "We had all climbed onto the wagon and were about to head out when Lucy jumped down and ran back into the house. I think she wanted to fetch her doll."

"Oh." Amy patted her waistband. The doll was still there. She pulled the sodden toy from her pants and handed it to the girl. "Here."

Lucinda wrapped her arms around the doll and clutched it to her chest, mud and all.

Amy felt hands on her shoulders. She turned.

Her parents were standing behind her with Nattie and Hannah.

"Come on," Papa said. "Let's go home."

* * *

"Weren't you scared?" Hannah whispered.

Amy turned in bed to face Hannah. "A little." She kept her voice low too so she wouldn't wake Nattie, who had bedded down next to Amy's bed while the Buchanans slept in her room.

"Climbing into the house even though you can't swim was really brave," Hannah said. "You saved little Lucy."

She threw her arms around Amy, pressing their chemise-clad bodies together, and planted a kiss on Amy's cheek.

Heat rushed through Amy. Her body tingled. She lay still, barely daring to breathe. Basking in the glow of Hannah's admiration, she felt six feet tall.

Hannah didn't pull back. She laid her head on Amy's shoulder and sighed dreamily.

Oh, Lord. This has got to be the best moment in my life.

"Amy?" Hannah whispered.

Amy's breath caught. What was Hannah about to say? She tried to make out Hannah's expression in the darkness but couldn't. "Yes?"

"Joshua finally asked me."

Joshua? Why was Hannah talking about Joshua now? "Asked you what?"

Hannah lifted her head off Amy's shoulder and leaned over her on one elbow. "He asked me to marry him." Her teeth gleamed in the moonlight as she smiled. "And I said yes."

Amy's moment of happiness crumpled just as the Buchanans' house had disintegrated around her. She felt as if she were going to be sick. "M-marry?"

"Yes," Hannah said. "Isn't it great?"

"B-but ..." Amy shook her head. "Why now?" Joshua had been courting Hannah for some time, but Amy had never thought about them marrying. She had imagined she would spend summers riding the range with Hannah forever. "Maybe you should wait."

Hannah sat up. "Wait? Amy, I'm almost nineteen. My brother and sister were married and had a child when they were my age." She leaned over Amy and looked into her eyes. "You don't think marrying Josh is a good idea? I really care for him."

"I know," Amy said. For the last two years, Hannah had gone on and on about how wonderful Joshua was and how he made her heart race and her stomach flutter whenever he was close. Finally, it had dawned on Amy that Hannah could have been describing Amy's feelings for her. Amy let her head sink back onto the pillow. "But what about ...?"

"About what?"

"What about me?" Amy whispered.

Hannah hugged her again. "Oh, Amy. Just because I'm getting married doesn't mean we can't be friends anymore. Soon you'll be all grown up, and you'll fall in love with a wonderful man and marry too. Maybe one day, our children will grow up together."

"I don't think so."

Hannah patted her arm. "You just wait and see."

Amy didn't answer.

"What is it?" Hannah asked. "What's wrong?"

Amy shrugged. She couldn't explain what she barely understood herself, least of all to Hannah.

"Let's go to sleep," Hannah said after a minute. "Your parents said we'll head over to the Buchanans' farm in the morning. Maybe there's something we can save from the outbuildings. Sleep well."

"You too," Amy mumbled. She turned her back toward Hannah and stared into the darkness, feeling as if she were still in the floating house, with the world spinning around her. After a while, she realized Hannah had fallen asleep. Quietly, she slipped out of bed, stepped over the softly snoring Nattie, and tiptoed downstairs. Maybe a visit to the stable would help clear her head.

The bottom step creaked before Amy reached it.

Amy paused. Was someone else awake?

"Mama?" a small voice asked.

"No, Lucy. It's me—Amy. What are you doing up?" Now that her eyes had grown more used to the darkness, she could see Lucinda huddled on the bottom step. Had the girl had a nightmare? After what she had been through, Amy wouldn't be surprised. She took Lucinda's hand and led her into the parlor, where she lit a kerosene lamp.

Lucinda clutched her still damp-looking doll and stared up at Amy with adoration. "Thank you for bringing Betty back."

"You're very welcome," Amy said, keeping her voice low so she wouldn't wake the Garfields, who were sleeping in the parlor. She tapped the doll's porcelain nose. "I had a doll just like this when I was little." Sometimes, she longed for those days, when she and Hannah had run along the wagons traveling to Oregon, or later, when they had held hands as they watched a foal being born. When had her innocent adoration of her older friend turned into these strange, confusing feelings?

"What happened to her?" Lucinda asked.

Amy glanced down at her. "Um, what?"

"What happened to your doll?"

"She fell into a river," Amy said.

"Oh." Lucinda clutched her doll more tightly against her chest. "Did you get another one?"

Amy shook her head. "No. Back then, we didn't have much money, and on the journey to Oregon, there were no stores to buy a new doll."

Chewing her lip, Lucinda looked back and forth between her doll and Amy. Finally, she held the doll out to Amy. "I give you mine."

Amy blinked. This little girl had lost her home and nearly her life, yet she offered to give up the only thing she had left. *Compared to her, I've got so much.* She reached out and stroked Lucinda's head. "You keep it, sweetie. I don't need it. After I lost my doll, my papa made toy horses for me."

Lucinda pulled the doll back against her chest. "I like horses."

"Me too," Amy said. "Want to go and visit the horses with me?" Spending time with the horses always helped her forget about her troubles for a while. Maybe it would do the same for Lucinda. Amy held out her hand.

Lucinda hesitated. "The horses' home won't swim away, will it?"

"No, Lucy. It won't. So, shall we go?"

Nodding eagerly, Lucinda took Amy's hand.

They tiptoed through the parlor, where Jacob was snoring on the sofa, his feet hanging off the end. When they stepped onto the porch, the rain had finally stopped, and for the first time in weeks, the moon wasn't hiding behind clouds. An owl hooted in the pine tree behind the house.

Amy lifted her face to the sky and breathed in the night air.

Lucinda tugged on her hand.

Smiling, Amy led her toward the stable. No matter what the future would bring, she would have her family and the horses. If that was enough for a little girl like Lucinda, it would be enough for her too.

###

EXCERPT FROM *BACKWARDS TO OREGON*
by Jae

Independence, Missouri,
April 27th, 1851

Rough laughter and the thumping of booted feet across the boardwalk made Tess look up.

"Soldiers." Fleur groaned next to her before the first of them had even entered. In the three years that the young woman had worked for Tess, she had learned a lot about men—even identifying their profession by their footfalls.

"Don't sound so snide, girl," Tess said. "Last time, they left you a nice tip."

"Last time, they also left me a nice black eye."

True. After long months of living in the shabby barracks of a secluded fort, with no break from their monotonous duties and bad food, soldiers tended to go a little wild on payday. "I'll keep an eye on them," Tess said.

The door swung open. Loud voices and fresh air drifted into the brothel's parlor, and for a moment, the smoke dispersed.

Tess stepped forward to extend a flirtatious greeting, but her well-practiced business smile gave way to a delighted laugh when she saw the last man being dragged in by his comrades.

Luke Hamilton was no longer the girl she had been

five years ago. She had returned from Mexico after fighting for more than a year, wounded, commissioned on the battlefield to the rank of lieutenant, and more reserved than ever. The war had changed her. Tess had fought hard to break through that shield of bitter aloofness, and though Luke had shared her bed in the aftermath of the war, she had never really shared her thoughts and emotions.

"Well, well, well, if it isn't Lieutenant Luke Hamilton, visiting a house of ill repute," Tess said. "Finally gotten lonely, soldier?"

Her visitor took off a wide-brimmed hat and smiled down at Tess. "I'm no longer a soldier."

"What?" For the first time, Tess noticed that Luke's navy-blue uniform had been replaced by worn civilian clothes.

"I've resigned my commission," Luke said. "My soldiering days are over."

Tess blinked. "How long have you been planning that?"

Luke looked down, studying the tips of her scuffed boots. "A while."

She hadn't mentioned anything on her last payday, and for a moment, that hurt, but then Tess reminded herself of her role. She was Luke's friend and occasional lover, nothing more.

"So what are you gonna do now?" Tess asked. "You got a position in town somewhere?"

Luke shook her head. "I'm gonna be my own man now."

It was no longer strange for Tess to hear Luke refer to herself as a man.

"I'll head west in a few days," Luke said.

"West? Don't tell me you've contracted that gold

fever?"

Luke smiled. "Lord, no. I prefer working with horses to digging in the mud. The Donation Land Claim Act grants one hundred and sixty acres of land to every male citizen," she grinned at Tess, "and I hear the Oregon Territory would be a good place for a horse ranch."

"So you're leaving for good?" Tess bit her lip. She was sad to see Luke go because she was a friend and one of very few people who had always treated her like a respectable woman.

"Yes. As soon as the grass grows long enough that the oxen won't starve on the way. Some of the boys dragged me in here for a memorable good-bye. I was wondering if you might be free tonight." Luke looked up at her through dark lashes. A rare shy smile appeared on Luke's lips.

Tess rubbed her forehead and sighed. "No, I'm not."

"Oh. All right." Luke was fast to hide her disappointment, as reluctant to show her feelings as ever.

Tess touched her hand to establish some kind of contact and prevent her younger friend from pulling away. "I'm sorry. If I could somehow—"

"No." Luke squeezed her hand for a second. "You've got nothing to apologize for. You need to make a living. I know that."

Suppressing another sigh, Tess signaled Charlie to pour Luke a whiskey. "I have to go and play the charming hostess now, but I'll make sure to see you before you leave, all right?" Tess made her way to the back of the room, greeting customers left and right. She stopped when she felt some gold dollars being shoved into her hand. "I'm sorry, but I'm already otherwise engaged tonight. Why don't you—?"

The bearded soldier laughed. "I wasn't asking for

myself. I want the services of your best girl for my friend over there." He pointed to the bar. "He's leaving town in a few days, and I want him to have a memorable send-off."

Tess looked down at the money in her hand. "Must be some friend," she said with her well-practiced flirtatious smile.

"He saved my life twice. So, you'll arrange it?"

Tess nodded. "Just point him out, and I'll see to it."

The soldier turned and indicated—Luke Hamilton.

Great. Tess mentally rolled her eyes. *How do I get you out of this one, my friend?* She was the only one Luke had ever trusted with her body and her secret, so she couldn't very well send her off with one of her girls. But she also couldn't ignore the bearded soldier's request. Every unmarried man in town would jump at the chance to spend a few hours with a working girl for free, especially if it would be months until he saw another available woman. Refusing the generous offer would make Luke's friends suspicious and could blow her cover. *And I want to give her a memorable send-off too.* She nodded at the bearded soldier. "I'll make sure he has a good time."

"Thank you." The soldier walked away.

The question is just how. Deeply in thought, Tess looked up—and right into the forest green eyes of a girl passing by. *That's it.* "Fleur," she called.

Out of the twelve girls working for her, Fleur was the one Tess trusted the most. At twenty, Fleur was only ten years younger than Tess, but she was like a daughter nonetheless. With her flaming red hair and her pretty, innocent face, she was popular with the men and brought in a lot of money for the establishment, but Tess hoped that she'd one day leave to begin a new life. She genuinely liked the young woman.

Fleur casually disengaged herself from the man she had been leading toward the bar and stopped in front of Tess. "Yes?"

"Are you about to head upstairs?"

Fleur looked back at her customer, who had already found another girl. "Doesn't look like it."

Tess hesitated for another moment, gazing deeply into Fleur's eyes. She knew that Fleur was very discreet. Unlike some of the other girls who gossiped whenever they thought Tess wasn't listening, Fleur never talked about what she did upstairs or about the secrets her customers might have let slip in the heat of passion. She was kind enough not to laugh at Luke and experienced enough not to run from the room screaming. And Luke would surely appreciate her soft beauty and feminine curves. In some respects, her friend was not so different from the man she pretended to be. "I have a customer I want you to take care of. The fee is already covered. He's a friend of mine, so please treat him well."

Fleur tilted her head. "Are you sure you don't want to entertain him yourself?"

"I would, but I have to entertain a town official tonight." Tess exchanged a meaningful glance with Fleur. The local authorities were willing to turn their heads in exchange for a few favors. For the most part, Tess as the madam of the brothel could pick her customers and saw only a few special guests, but she had no choice tonight. She had to ensure that town officials continued to turn a blind eye to her establishment.

"And the one you want me to take care of? Is he a regular?" Fleur asked.

Tess shook her head. "No. But he's special, so I don't trust any of the other girls to take care of him."

Fleur turned to look in the same direction Tess did. "The dark-haired, slender one standing alone at the bar? He doesn't look like one of your special customers."

A smile played around Tess's lips. "Oh, he is special, trust me." She turned toward Fleur and looked her in the eyes, her smile now gone. "You still remember the first rule I taught you?"

"Don't steal your silverware?" Fleur said with the mischievous grin she still hadn't lost completely after three years.

Tess suppressed a smile of her own. "Discretion."

A russet eyebrow rose, but Fleur didn't ask what it was about this customer that required her absolute discretion. After a few seconds, she asked, "Is there anything I should be careful about?" A glimmer of fearful caution shone in her green eyes.

"No." Tess shook her head. "You've got nothing to fear from him. He's a real gentleman."

One corner of Fleur's lips lifted into a humorless half-smile. "That would be a first. But all right. I'll take care of him." She turned and made her way toward the bar.

"I hope I did the right thing," Tess whispered as she watched her go.

The revised and expanded edition of *Backwards to Oregon* is now available at many online bookstores as an e-book and in print.

ABOUT JAE

Jae grew up amidst the vineyards of southern Germany. She spent her childhood with her nose buried in a book, earning her the nickname "professor." The writing bug bit her at the age of eleven. For the last six years, she has been writing mostly in English.

She works as a psychologist and likes to spend her time reading, playing board games with friends, spending time with her nieces and nephew, and watching way too many crime shows.

Connect with Jae online

Jae loves hearing from readers!
E-mail her at jae_s1978@yahoo.de
Visit her blog: jaefiction.wordpress.com
Visit her website: jae-fiction.com
Follow her on Twitter @jaefiction

Backwards to Oregon
(revised and expanded edition)
Jae

"Luke" Hamilton has always been sure that she'd never marry. She accepted that she would spend her life alone when she chose to live her life disguised as a man.

After working in a brothel for three years, Nora Macauley has lost all illusions about love. She no longer hopes for a man who will sweep her off her feet and take her away to begin a new, respectable life.

But now they find themselves married and on the way to Oregon in a covered wagon, with two thousand miles ahead of them.

Something in the Wine
Jae

All her life, Annie Prideaux has suffered through her brother's constant practical jokes only he thinks are funny. But Jake's last joke is one too many, she decides when he sets her up on a blind date with his friend Drew Corbin—neglecting to tell his straight sister one tiny detail: her date is not a man, but a lesbian.

Annie and Drew decide it's time to turn the tables on Jake by pretending to fall in love with each other.

At first glance, they have nothing in common. Disillusioned with love, Annie focuses on books, her cat, and her work as an accountant while Drew, more confident and outgoing, owns a dog and spends most of her time working in her beloved vineyard.

Only their common goal to take revenge on Jake unites them. But what starts as a table-turning game soon turns Annie's and Drew's lives upside down as the lines between pretending and reality begin to blur.

Hot Line
Alison Grey

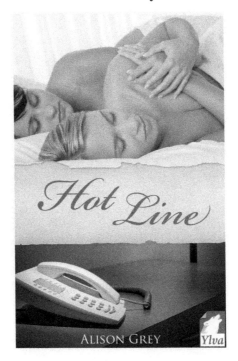

Two women from different worlds. Linda, a successful psychologist, uses her work to distance herself from her own loneliness.

Christina works for a sex hotline to make ends meet.

Their worlds collide when Linda calls Christina's sex line. Christina quickly realizes Linda is not her usual customer. Instead of wanting phone sex, Linda makes an unexpected proposition. Does Christina dare accept the offer that will change both their lives?

L.A. Metro
RJ Nolan

Dr. Kimberly Donovan's life is in shambles. After her medical ethics are questioned, first her family, then her closeted lover, the Chief of the ER, betray her. Determined to make a fresh start, she flees to California and L.A. Metropolitan Hospital.

Dr. Jess McKenna, L.A. Metro's Chief of the ER, gives new meaning to the phrase emotionally guarded, but she has her reasons.

When Kim and Jess meet, the attraction is immediate. Emotions Jess has tried to repress for years surface. But her interest in Kim also stirs dark memories. They settle for friendship, determined not to repeat past mistakes, but secretly they both wish things could be different.

Will the demons from the past destroy their future before it can even get started? Or will L.A. Metro be a place to not only heal the sick, but to mend wounded hearts?

Manhattan Moon
Jae

Nothing in Shelby Carson's life is ordinary. Not only is she an attending psychiatrist in a hectic ER, but she's also a Wrasa, a shape-shifter who leads a secret existence.

To make things even more complicated, she has feelings for Nyla Rozakis, a human nurse.

Even though the Wrasa forbid relationships with humans, Shelby is determined to pursue Nyla. Things seem pretty hopeless for them, but on Halloween, during a full moon, anything can happen...

Connected Hearts
Jae, RJ Nolan, Joan Arling

Four romantic short stories:

The Morning After by Jae

After a friend sets her up on a blind date from hell, Amanda has enough of dating. A spur-of-the-moment decision to attend an Anti-Valentine's Day party leads to an unexpected encounter. She wakes up to a hangover and a surprising complication...

Two Hearts—One Mind by RJ Nolan

Kim is a woman on a mission: She wants to propose to her partner, Jess, on Valentine's Day. But things don't turn out as planned, because Jess has a plan of her own...

On the Road by Joan Arling

Stella, a long-haul trucker, picks up a hitchhiker on her way south across Europe. Long before reaching Sicily, she falls for her passenger, Rita. Stella is thrilled when she learns that Rita returns her feelings. But because of her job, there seems to be no way for them to be together.

Seduction for Beginners by Jae

For Annie, work always took precedence over romance. But now, recently come-out and involved in a relationship with a woman for the first time, Annie is determined to seduce her girlfriend, Drew, on Valentine's Day. Unfortunately, she has no clue as to the arts of seduction.

Walking the Labyrinth
Lois Cloarec Hart

Is there life after loss? Lee Glenn, co-owner of a private security company, didn't think so. Crushed by grief after the death of her wife, she uncharacteristically retreats from life.

But love doesn't give up easily. After her friends and family stage a dramatic intervention, Lee rejoins the world of the living, resolved to regain some sense of normalcy but only half-believing that it's possible. Her old friend and business partner convinces her to take on what appears on the surface to be a minor personal protection detail.

The assignment takes her far from home, from the darkness of her loss to the dawning of a life reborn. Along the way, Lee encounters people unlike any she's ever met before: Wrong-Way Wally, a small-town oracle shunned by the locals for his off-putting speech and mannerisms; and Wally's best friend, Gaëlle, a woman who not only translates the oracle's uncanny predictions, but who also appears to have a deep personal connection to life beyond life. Lee is shocked to find herself fascinated by Gaëlle, despite dismissing the woman's exotic beliefs as "hooey."

But opening yourself to love also means opening yourself to the possibility of pain. Will Lee have the courage to follow that path, a path that once led to the greatest agony she'd ever experienced? Or will she run back to the cold comfort of a safer solitary life?

Crossing Bridges
Emma Weimann

As a Guardian, Tallulah has devoted her life to protecting her hometown, Edinburgh, and its inhabitants, both living and dead, against ill-natured and dangerous supernatural beings.

When Erin, a human tourist, visits Edinburgh, she makes Tallulah more nervous than the poltergeist on Greyfriars Kirkyard—and not only because Erin seems to be the sidekick of a dark witch who has her own agenda.

While Tallulah works to thwart the dark witch's sinister plan for Edinburgh, she can't help wondering about the mysterious Erin. Is she friend or foe?

Second Nature
(revised edition)
Jae

Novelist Jorie Price doesn't believe in the existence of shape-shifting creatures or true love. She leads a solitary life, and the paranormal romances she writes are pure fiction for her.

Griffin Westmore knows better—at least about one of these two things. She doesn't believe in love either, but she's one of the not-so-fictional shape-shifters. She's also a Saru, an elite soldier with the mission to protect the shape-shifters' secret existence at any cost.

When Jorie gets too close to the truth in her latest shape-shifter romance, Griffin is sent to investigate—and if necessary to destroy the manuscript before it's published and to kill the writer.

See Right Through Me
L. T. Smith

Trust, respect, and love. Three little words—that's all. But these words are powerful, and if we ignore any one of them, then three other little words take their place: jealousy, insecurity, and heartbreak.

School teacher Gemma Hughes is an ordinary woman living an ordinary life. Disorganized and clumsy, she soon finds herself in the capable hands of the beautiful Dr. Maria Moran. Everything goes wonderfully until Gemma starts doubting Maria's intentions and begins listening to the wrong people.

But has Maria something to hide, or is it a case of swapping trust for insecurity, respect for jealousy and finishing with a world of heartbreak and deceit? Can Gemma stop her actions before it's too late? Or will she ruin the best thing to happen in her life?

Given her track record, anything is possible.

Ingram Content Group UK Ltd.
Milton Keynes UK
UKHW042209080323
418239UK00001B/255